Road Stories

Novellas

Lou Mindar

Driftless House Publishing

This book is a work of fiction. Any reference to historical events, real people, or real places are used fictitiously. Other names, characters, places, and events are products of the author's imagination, and any resemblance to actual events or places or persons, living or dead, is entirely coincidental.

Library of Congress Cataloging-in-Publication Data
Mindar, Lou (1959 -)
Road Stories / Lou Mindar. – First Edition.
[Novellas]
Pages cm
ISBN 978-0-9972488-0-7
Paperback edition

for Shelby and Louis

Contents

Road Stories

Tierra del Fuego

A misty rain fell as we made our way through the early morning darkness. Our little Peugot climbed steep, muddy roads toward the ferry we hoped would be waiting for us on the other side of the mountain. Sebastian was behind the wheel, awake and alert. I was crumpled in the passenger seat, trying to sleep, but the jostling and jarring from the car hitting puddled ruts in the road kept me awake.

We'd left Sebastian's farm, *Finca Fin del Mundo*, at four o'clock that morning. The farm sat in the hills several miles north of Ushuaia, the capital city of the province of Tierra del Fuego, and the southernmost city in Argentina. It was April in Tierra del Fuego, autumn in the Southern Hemisphere. The weather was cold and rainy, the air smelling of earthy decay.

Sebastian had both hands on the wheel, his sad, friendly eyes fixed on the narrow road ahead. I marveled to think that a month earlier I hadn't even known him. We'd met as strangers, pushed together by circumstances, and were about to part as friends, knowing that we were unlikely to ever see each other again. His finca had been a safe, albeit unlikely, landing spot for me, and I hated to leave. The thought of simply staying had crossed my mind several times, but I knew I had to go.

Sebastian's small car struggled to gain traction going up the muddy mountain road. Several times he had to shift to a lower gear to keep moving forward. The car never faltered, and a little over an hour after we began our journey, we descended the other side of the mountain on our way toward Rio Grande.

The rain fell harder on the way down the mountain and the muddy road became slicker and more treacherous. I was nervous, but Sebastian handled the road with the ease of a seasoned veteran. He was calm, having grown up in these conditions, while I sweated every twist and turn.

The sun climbed in the eastern sky as we made our way down the mountain and I saw cloud-muted rays glinting off the surface of a large lake in the distance.

"What is that?" I asked.

"That's Lake Fagnano. It is named after Monsignor Fagnano, the Italian priest who came to Tierra del Fuego many years ago to protect the natives who were living here at the time."

"It looks pretty big."

"Oh, yes. It's very long. We will be driving on the south and east side of the lake. It goes all the way to the west into Chile. You should see it on a sunny day. It is beautiful."

Although Lake Fagnano was much smaller, it reminded me of Lake Michigan and my home in Chicago. And I couldn't think of home without thinking of my wife, Lisa, dead now for more than three months. A trickle of sweat ran down my back. I unzipped my coat and struggled to get comfortable in my seat. I tried not to think about Lisa, but I found it was impossible.

We drove for quite some time under overcast skies with the lake on our left. We were now on flat ground and there were tall trees on either side of the road. Sebastian pointed out lenga and coihue trees as we drove past the thick forests. One type was tall, maybe eighty or a hundred feet in height, with a high canopy filled with red and yellow leaves. The other was even taller with flat, elegant branches, and green leaves. I didn't know which of the trees corresponded to which of the names Sebastian was saying, so I mostly just nodded as he spoke.

Away from the lake, the terrain turned rocky and barren. The trees gave way to a world that was flat, brown and muddy, punctuated by the occasional tuft of grass or bush with tiny white and yellow flowers. The sun was well up in the sky now, but thick clouds blocked much of its light. Off to our right, a curious guanaco, about the size of a large deer, with a coat of tan and white, chewed its cud as it watched us go by.

Sebastian was quiet as we drove through the desolate surroundings. I thought about leaving the sanctuary of Tierra del Fuego and returning home. I knew that all of the things that reminded me of Lisa would be there—her clothes, the furniture she picked out, photos of us together—but Lisa wouldn't. The house would be the same, our friends would be the same, the business I owned with my brother would be the same, but without Lisa, nothing would be the same. I fought the urge to have Sebastian turn the car around so we could return to the refuge of the finca.

§

After the funeral, I was catatonic. I showed up to business meetings, went to the gym, and joined friends for dinner, but in body only. I listened to people talk, but what they said didn't register. I nodded a lot but usually didn't know why. In the middle of conversations I politely excused myself, even though I didn't have anywhere else to be.

A couple of weeks after the funeral, I was out to dinner with my brother, Scott, at Girl and the Goat, one of my favorite restaurants. I had ordered the grilled marinated pork belly, but was just moving it around my plate, my appetite having all but abandoned me. My brother had just ordered another round of drinks when Don and Trish Davenport, friends of our parents, stopped by our table.

"How are you doing?" Trish asked, placing her hand on my shoulder. She tilted her head and scrunched up the corner of her mouth after asking the question, her eyes wide with concern.

I had been asked the question hundreds of times over the previous two weeks, and I never knew how to answer it. Did they want to know the truth, that I felt like I was dying inside? No, that would be too uncomfortable.

"I'm doing okay, Trish."

"That's good. We were just so sorry to hear about what happened."

I thanked her, and then excused myself, claiming I had to use the bathroom. I couldn't handle the seemingly endless condolences.

At the commercial real estate management company I owned with my brother, I took to sitting in my office with the door closed. I refused to take any calls, instead having my assistant tell people I would call them back. Even so, I didn't return the phone calls. When our clients began to complain, my brother Scott returned the phone messages meant for me. After a few days of this, he had all of my calls routed to his office and generously told me I should just go home.

Being away from the demands of my office didn't help. At home, I was surrounded by all of the things I shared with Lisa, and everything reminded me of her. The Keurig coffee maker reminded me of how we used to sit out on the deck sipping coffee on warm summer mornings. The TV brought back memories of the nights we spent snuggled on the couch with a bowl of popcorn watching movies. Even our CRU Lauderdale dinnerware reminded me of the day we spent before our wedding picking out the perfect plates and bowls. The pattern we chose was important to Lisa, so it was important to me.

There were other memories too that I couldn't avoid by being at home. I remembered the strange way Lisa started acting around me. It was little things. She spent more and more time at the office. When she came home late, she often fell asleep on the couch or went to bed early rather than sitting and talking to me the way she used to. She didn't laugh as often, she seemed to stiffen at my touch, and, although she said it was just in my mind, I swear she tried to avoid being in the same room with me.

There were more specific things too. Lisa bought new clothes, sexy clothes, in the weeks before her death. She began wearing jewelry I wasn't familiar with, and she had her nails done. I checked her cell phone to see who she had been texting, but all of her texts had been erased.

A couple of weeks after the New Year, we had an ice storm and I left work early so I could get home before the worst of the storm hit. I spoke to Lisa earlier in the day and she too had agreed to leave her office early. When I got home, she wasn't there. There was no answer when I called her cell. When I called her office I was surprised she was still at work.

"I thought you were going to leave early," I said.

"I just have a couple of things to finish up," she said. "I'll leave in a little bit."

"The roads are getting bad. You really need to leave now to avoid the worst of it."

"I will," she said, but it was clear she didn't plan on leaving right away.

"What's going on, Lisa?"

"I'll be home, Matt. Just not now." Lisa was speaking in that low, controlled voice she used when she was trying to avoid saying something she didn't want to say.

"Come on, Lisa."

The phone was quiet for several moments before Lisa said, "I can't talk about this right now. I promise, I'll explain it to you when I get home."

She never made it home. That was the night she died in the accident. I sat on the couch waiting for her, wondering what it was she had to tell me. I was pretty sure I knew the short version. Things had changed and Lisa wanted out of the marriage. I wasn't sure about the specifics, but I had felt the pending doom of divorce hanging in the air for some time. But why? What had happened? How had things changed? I was still asking myself those same questions weeks after the funeral when I was once again sitting at home by myself.

My brother told me to go home, to relax and deal with my grief, but I couldn't relax and I had no idea how to deal with grief. The same questions I asked myself on the night Lisa died still consumed me. What was it that Lisa was keeping from me? I couldn't stand being home alone with my thoughts and I couldn't function at work. I had nowhere to go, but I had to get away.

The last straw was dealing with Lisa's life insurance. She had a policy through her office that paid five hundred thousand dollars. I was stunned. We had never discussed our life insurance needs and I didn't expect to walk away with a bunch of money after Lisa's death. Why should I get hundreds of thousands of dollars just because my wife died before she could divorce me? There was a part of me that felt lucky she had died before she could tell me she was having an affair, but the second I felt lucky, I immediately hated myself for the feeling. I couldn't take it anymore. I stuck the money in the bank, packed a suitcase, locked the door behind me, and drove away from my home and my life.

§

I was just about to cross the Mississippi River heading into St. Louis when my phone rang. It was my brother. I didn't answer. I told myself it was because I needed both hands on the wheel of my Audi as I crossed the bridge, but the truth was that I wasn't in the mood to talk to him or anyone else.

I tried to focus my attention straight ahead on the road, but the swirling, eddying water below me drew my attention downward. My whole life, I had dealt with a fear of bridges over water. Bridges over railroad tracks or other roads didn't bother me, and being on the water, either swimming or out on a boat, wasn't a problem. But put me near or over water in a car, and I'd fill with trepidation. As I drove into Missouri, the river behind me and the Gateway Arch disappearing off to my right, I realized I had been holding my breath. I refocused on the roadway, and followed the midday traffic through the city.

I stopped near Sullivan, Missouri on I-44 to get gas and eat. I listened to Scott's message while waiting for my food.

"Hey, it's me. I'm just checking in to see how you're doing. Give me a call."

I didn't call back. After a couple of bites of my burger, I re-wrapped it and tossed it back in the bag.

I drove mindlessly, listening to the radio, reading billboards, comparing gas prices, but no matter what I did, I couldn't stop thinking about Lisa. Between Springfield and Joplin, Scott called again and left another message.

"Hey, where are you? I'm getting concerned. Call me when you get this message," the voice on my voicemail said.

Without giving it any thought, I set the GPS for Dallas and then did what the little electronic box told me to do. When the robotic voice told me to turn off of I-44 onto U.S. 69, that's what I did. Then it said to turn onto U.S. 75 and I did as I was told. If the GPS said it, I did it.

I knew that, at one time, Lisa and I had been very much in love. We spent as much time together as possible, and couldn't be separated for more than a few hours without checking in by phone. When we were together, we always had to be touching each other, whether we were out for a walk, or driving in the car, or sitting next to each other at dinner or a movie.

As I drove, I remembered back to a time early in our marriage when we spent a long weekend at a lake cabin in Wisconsin. We spent the morning rafting a local river and we returned to the cabin where we took a nap and ended up making love late into the afternoon. We showered together and then went out for a romantic dinner. When we returned to the cabin, I poured each of us a glass of wine, and Lisa cuddled up next to me on the leather sofa. We listened to soft music as we watched the fire in the cabin's stone fireplace.

"I want things to stay like this forever," Lisa said.

"Wouldn't that be nice?"

"I don't mean just here at the cabin with the music and the wine. I want us to stay close and in love. I want us to always be together."

But things changed after those early days of our marriage. Lisa changed. I thought back to the night before Lisa's death. She had spent much of the evening on the phone in our bedroom with the door closed. When she came back out into the living room where I was watching TV, she fell asleep on the couch without talking to me. When I was ready to go to bed, I woke her and tried to coax her into the bedroom, but she just fell back to sleep on the couch and slept there all night. This had become fairly commonplace.

My feelings for Lisa hadn't changed. I was still in love with her and wanted to be with her all of the time, but at some point, things had changed for Lisa. As I drove, I wondered when they had changed, and why.

§

Somewhere north of Dallas I started to feel sleepy, and decided to get a room for the night. Scott called two more times and left a message each time. With each message, his tone became more and more worried. I went to bed without returning his calls.

To my surprise, I slept pretty well at the hotel. I had been exhausted, and I was grateful for the good night's sleep, but I woke up thinking about Scott and how worried he was about me. It wasn't fair of me to ignore his messages. He was covering for me at work. The least I could do was return his phone calls.

I stopped at a Dunkin Donuts thinking I could avoid the morning rush hour traffic while having breakfast. I sipped coffee in a booth by myself and called Scott.

"Matt, where are you?"

"Hi to you, too," I said. "I'm in Texas."

"God, what are you doing down there? Are you okay?"

"I'm fine, and I'm not really sure what I'm doing down here. Mostly I'm just driving."

Scott started to speak, but stopped. There was a moment of silence and he said, "Seriously, Matt, what are you doing down there? When are you coming home?"

“I don’t know. I can’t be at home right now. I just need to get away for a little bit.”

There was more silence and then Scott said, “Okay, I guess, if you need to get away. Just be careful. Let me hear from you so I know where you are, okay?”

I promised to keep in touch and hung up. I felt the trapped, constrained feeling of home starting to creep in on me again, so I got up from the booth, leaving my donuts on the table, and walked out to my car. I punched San Antonio into the GPS and got back on the road.

§

I crossed into Mexico on the Pharr International Bridge where I-69C turns into Mexico Route 97 near Reynoso. The low-slung bridge didn’t bother me the way the taller bridges did. I had never before been to Mexico, and I couldn’t help but see the irony in Lisa’s death pushing me to leave the country. Early in our marriage, Lisa wanted to travel outside the United States, but I had balked at the idea. The thought of leaving the country was discomforting. You couldn’t drink the water in other countries, you had to look out for thieves and rip-off artists, the hotels were overpriced, the people unfriendly. Lisa persisted. I went so far as to get a passport, but I never used it. I just couldn’t get past my irrational fears.

I had heard horror stories about Americans traveling in Mexico, but I found it wasn’t much different than traveling in the United States. When I needed gas, I stopped at a gas station. When I was hungry, I pulled into a restaurant. And when I got tired, I stopped for the night. That first night I made it to Heroica Veracruz, a city on the Gulf of Mexico. I stayed at a Holiday Inn. It was as if I had never left the U.S.

The next morning I left Heroica Veracruz and drove across the narrowest part of Mexico, crossing from the Gulf to the Pacific Coast and onto Mexico Route 200. Near Tapachula, I stopped for gas before I crossed

into Guatemala. As I stood at the pump filling the tank of my car, a man approached me and said something in Spanish. He wore faded blue pants that were too short for him and a dirty red t-shirt. He had what looked like homemade sandals on his feet, constructed from rope and duct tape.

"I don't speak Spanish," I said.

The man seemingly didn't speak English because he repeated what he had said earlier, but this time more loudly and with his hand extended. His meaning was clear. He wanted money.

I pulled a ten out of my pocket and handed it to him. Without looking at the money, he stuffed it in his pocket and walked away.

A man filling his car at the next pump looked at me and shook his head. "Why do you give him money?" he asked with an accent. "That just encourages them." He was dressed in a black and gold polo shirt and pumped gas into a late model Mercedes.

I shrugged, feeling lost and stupid.

"Where are you heading, Amigo?" the man asked.

I had to think about his question for a second. I wasn't going anywhere in particular. I was just heading south. "To Costa Rica," I said, not at all sure of myself.

"It is not a good idea to drive through Guatemala at night. I would suggest you get a room here in Tapachula tonight and then drive into Honduras in the daylight. I wouldn't drive in Honduras at night either if I was you."

"Thanks. I appreciate the advice," I said. What was I doing down here? Everything had gone fine so far, but it sounded like I was driving toward more dangerous territory. I thought about just turning around and heading back to the safety of home, but the idea filled me with dread. I decided to follow the advice I had been given, and get a room in Tapachula where I could consider my options.

I ended up at the Hotel Don Miguel on Calle Poniente near Central Park in the middle of town. The room was simple with a queen size bed and a small table with two chairs. It served my purposes. It was late afternoon and I decided to take a short nap.

When I awoke it was dark and I wasn't sure where I was. An indistinct dream about Lisa filled my mind. As the dream faded, it took me a few dazed seconds to get my bearings and then to find the switch for the light next to the bed. I looked at my watch. It was five minutes past nine. I was groggy, so I went into the bathroom to splash my face. My stomach growled and I thought about ordering room service, but I didn't want to be alone. The last few days in the car had been enough. I wanted to be around other people, as long as they didn't know me and didn't ask how I was doing after my wife's death.

The restaurant was called Los Jarrones and it was nicer than I expected. The waiters wore starched white shirts and bow ties, and the tables featured candles. Soft music floated down from speakers in the ceiling. A romantic dinner all by myself was not what I had in mind, but it was late and I was already there. A beautiful woman with light caramel skin, dark hair and a gold form-fitting dress welcomed me in English and led me to my table.

"Enjoy your dinner, sir," she said as I sat down. She walked away and a young waiter replaced her at my table. He spoke English fluently and seemed pleased that he had someone to wait on who did not speak his first language. He took my drink order and then quickly walked off.

As I looked over the menu, I realized that I had not eaten since breakfast in Heroica Veracruz that morning. When the waiter returned with my glass of merlot, I ordered a medium-rare steak adobo with Mexican rice and pinto beans. The waiter nodded approvingly as I ordered, thanked me, and then was off again.

The restaurant was about three-quarters full and I couldn't help but notice the number of couples. They held hands, talked quietly, and laughed at a joke one or the other had made. They were together enjoying each other's company, and I was alone. It felt miserable.

Lisa and I had been out to eat at a nice restaurant a few weeks before her accident. We sat quietly, not talking. Although sitting without speaking had become normal in recent months, it made me uncomfortable. We should be talking, I remember thinking. We should have things to say to each other. I forced the conversation. "I'd like us to take a few days off and get out of town. Maybe we could head down to Florida or go skiing in Colorado. I'd even be willing to go on a cruise if you want. I don't really care what we do, just as long as we can get away for a while."

Lisa stared at me for a moment, seemingly unsure of how to respond. I read the look on her face as saying that my suggestion had been the furthest thing from her mind and she needed a moment to decipher my words.

"That would be nice," she said, "but things are crazy at work right now and I don't think I can get away for a while." She looked down at her lap and didn't say anything more.

Lisa worked at a public relations firm and had always been serious and committed to her job, but earlier in our marriage, she had made time for me. In the months before her death, that had changed. I had been asking her for a while to take time off so we could have a vacation together—I was even willing to travel outside the U.S.—but she kept putting me off. She was always too busy at work. The time was never right.

"Is everything okay?" I asked, fearing the answer.

"Yeah, I'm just really busy," she said.

"Busy seeing someone else" went through my mind, but I didn't say it. I had always trusted Lisa, but something was going on and whatever it was, it was consistent with her having an affair.

I was jostled out of my memory when the waiter brought my meal and set it down in front of me. The rib eye steak was about half an inch thick and looked tender and juicy. It sat atop a mound of rice and pinto beans.

"Can I get you another glass of wine?" the waiter asked in perfect English.

"Yes. Thank you." I cut into the steak and took a bite. The taste of ancho chiles and lime juice filled my mouth and helped to take my mind off of the unpleasant memories. Despite the delicious meal, I lost my appetite after a few bites.

"Did you not enjoy your meal, Senor?" the waiter asked when he came to take my plate.

"It was delicious. I'm just full." I rested my hand on my stomach as if I couldn't eat another bite.

The waiter nodded. "May I ask you a question?"

"Of course," I said.

"I know you are from the United States, but from where?" he asked.

"I'm from Chicago."

"Ah, of course. I should have known. I went to university in Texas and I once traveled to Chicago for a weekend in the summer. I went to Wrigley Field and watched the Cubs play baseball. Sadly, they lost," he said.

"Yes, they do that a lot," I said. "Now, may I ask you a question?"

"Of course," he said with a smile.

"I was told earlier today that I should not drive through Guatemala or Honduras at night. Is this true or was the person who told me about this just trying to scare me?"

"I'm afraid he was telling you the truth, Senor. My uncle owns a home in Costa Rica near La Cruz and whenever we go down there, we only drive during the day. I have heard stories of robbers blocking the road and stopping cars to steal from them. I also heard of guerilla soldiers kidnapping foreigners and holding them for ransom. Driving at night in these countries is not a good idea."

Who would they contact if I was kidnapped? Who would pay the ransom?

The next morning I left early and drove through Guatemala to San Salvador, El Salvador. I only drove during the daylight hours and did the same thing the next day driving through Honduras to Managua, Nicaragua. I spent my days thinking about Lisa and looking for traps along the roadway. At night I tossed and turned, my dreams a confirmation of the thoughts I had all day of Lisa's betrayal.

I was grumpy and exhausted when I left Managua. I continued south through Costa Rica and into David, Panama, arriving about an hour before nightfall. When I pulled into the drive of the Cuidad de David Hotel, I was exhausted, but thankful that, except for a few crazy drivers, I had not met with any trouble during my trip.

Walking from the parking lot into the hotel, my body ached for sleep. I had spent my days driving as fast as the roads would permit to avoid a danger that may or may not have existed. At night, I was all keyed up and couldn't sleep. I remembered the way Lisa couldn't keep her hands off me in the early days of our marriage. She always had to be holding my hand or draping her arm around my shoulders. I thought about how when we were first married, Lisa would call me two or three times during the day just to check in, but how at the end, she rarely even had time to take my calls. The memories were exhausting and I needed a rest. I wasn't on a schedule and I wasn't even sure where I was going. There was no need to push myself. I was supposed to be relaxing, so I decided to stay in David for a couple of days.

Once in my room, I lay down on the bed and immediately fell asleep. I didn't even bother to take off the clothes I'd been wearing all day. I slept straight through the night and felt better upon waking than I had in several days. After taking a shower, I went down to the hotel restaurant for their complimentary breakfast buffet. I loaded up my plate and dug in. The eggs, breakfast meats, fruit, cereals, and pastries were delicious, and I gorged myself. I was surprised at my appetite. I still had some bacon and two small pastries on my plate when I decided I couldn't eat another bite.

"Looks like your eyes were bigger than your stomach," said the man sitting alone at the table next to me.

"I'm afraid so," I said. "Everything looks so good, but I'm stuffed."

"I know how you feel. I was the same way the first couple of times I stayed in the hotel." The man introduced himself as Ken Summers, an expat from California. He was tall and thin with wispy blond hair and the tanned skin of someone who spent a lot of time outdoors.

I told Ken I was from Chicago and asked, "Do you stay here often?"

"A couple of times a month," he said. "I live in Panama City, but I own some rental property here in David and up in the mountains in Boquete. I come over here to check on the properties and to visit with some of my expat friends. How about you? What brings you to David?" He pronounced it "Da-veed," with the accent on the second syllable.

"I'm just driving south and I ended up here last night," I said, only telling part of the story. "I'm going to stick around for a few days and take it easy."

Ken looked at me with knowing eyes, but just nodded his head, not saying anything.

"What goes on around here?" I asked, more to break the uncomfortable silence than because I was really interested.

"I'll tell you what," he said, "I have some business to take care of this morning, but how would you like to head up to Boquete with me this afternoon? There's a group of expats up there that gets together once a month. Today's the big day and I'd like you to join us. I think you'll have fun."

I thought back to a few nights earlier in Tapachula when I had wanted to be with other people only to end up feeling sorry for myself. But the truth was that I still found the idea of being around other people appealing. "Okay, sure," I said.

We made plans to meet and then Ken was gone to his appointment. I wasn't sure what the day held in store for me, but at least I wouldn't be spending it driving south with no purpose. I was looking forward to doing something different for a change.

While I waited for Ken, I went back to my room and called Scott. I had been out of touch for several days and I owed him a call. When he answered, his first question was, "Where are you?"

"I'm in Panama."

"Panama? The country?"

"Yes," I said. "I'm in David and plan on staying here for a couple of days."

"Are you okay?" he asked.

"Yeah, I'm okay, but I think Lisa was having an affair." The words jumped out of my mouth before I could stop them. I had never mentioned our marital troubles to Scott.

"Why do you think that?" he asked.

I told Scott about how Lisa had been avoiding me for the past few months; how she had gotten into the habit of falling asleep on the couch in the living room and staying there all night; how my overtures for sex had been met with evasion and excuses; and how she had, on the day she died, promised to tell me what was going on.

"That doesn't mean she was having an affair, Matt."

"There were other things too, Scott. That's all I've been thinking about while I've been on the road and I can't come up with a better explanation."

Scott was quiet for a moment and then said, "I just can't believe she would do that."

"Neither can I, but something was going on and not knowing is driving me crazy."

"Man, I don't know," Scott said, and then went quiet for a moment. "I hate to change the subject on you, but Greg Conover has been calling. The contract is up on his properties at the end of April and he wants to meet with you before then. I've put him off for now, but I'm not sure how long he's going to wait."

"Put Greg off for as long as you can," I said. "I'll deal with him later."

When I got off the phone, I felt like getting in my car and hitting the road again. The thoughts of home and the things that went on there made me want to run, to get as far away from Chicago and my life as possible. If I hadn't already made plans with Ken, I might have left. I desperately needed a distraction and I hoped that going to Boquete with Ken would provide it.

§

The road between David and Boquete was wide and newly paved. Ken told me that until recently, driving to Boquete was an adventure because you never knew for sure what condition the road would be in. Often, after rains, the road would be washed out. But now the trip was easy.

During the drive, I learned that Ken had moved to Panama three years earlier after his divorce. His son, his only child, was out of college and living in San Diego, so Ken flew back to California every couple of months to see him. Otherwise, he was perfectly happy living in Panama.

"I love this place," he told me. "It's like California was back in the fifties. Tons of opportunity and very few rules."

"What kind of opportunities?" I asked.

"Land and real estate is relatively inexpensive, especially compared to California. Tourists are really starting to flock here, so there are business opportunities with tourism. There's also money to be made with American franchises, although I happen to think we'd all be better off without them."

Once we got to Boquete, we drove off the main road to a home Ken owned. It was a simple one-story house with a small yard. "This is part of what I'm telling you. If I can keep my houses rented to tourists ten to fifteen weeks each year, the rent covers my expenses. But each of them is rented thirty to thirty-five weeks a year, so they're both making money for me. There's opportunity like this throughout the country."

As Ken talked, we pulled into a gravel parking lot in front of a small, yellow, one-story building. "Welcome to Mike's Global Grill," Ken said.

The low-roofed building had barred windows in the front, along with a wooden sign announcing that the restaurant offered international cuisine, live music, Wi-Fi, and sports. A large unchained dog lay in the shade of a purple-leafed bush at the front of the building, its tongue lolling in the heat. It ignored us when we got out of Ken's car.

I was surprised. I'd pictured a bigger place. Ken had described how good the food was and said that a lot of people would be there. From the outside, the restaurant looked run down and too small to hold many people. We were greeted by the man behind the bar.

"Hey, Ken. You're early," he said with a slight accent as he reached across the bar to shake Ken's hand.

"I wanted to get a good seat for the game." Ken turned toward me. "This is Matt Cravens. Matt, this is Enrique." I shook his hand. "Enrique is the bartender here, so he's your new best friend."

Ken ordered two bottles of Red Stripe, and Enrique said, "Don't you want to treat your friend here to a genuine Panamanian beer?"

"I wouldn't wish that piss water on anyone," Ken said, laughing.

Enrique looked hurt, but served the two Red Stripes, each with a foam koozie to keep the beers cold. We took our drinks out to a patio on the side of the building. "I thought we'd enjoy the sun for a while before people start showing up," he said.

We sat in brightly painted wooden Adirondack chairs with a small plastic table between us where we rested our beers. "What's wrong with the Panamanian beer?" I asked.

"It's not that bad," Ken said. "It's not great, but it's not horrible either. I just like Red Stripe, and I like to give Enrique a hard time."

I laughed and then we sat quietly listening to the sound of a small stream that ran along the side of the building only a few feet from the patio. The stream was clear and shallow, with riffles on the surface of the water where it ran over the uneven stream bottom. The sound was soothing, and I could feel my body relax into the chair in a way I had not felt in some time. We finished our beers, and Enrique brought fresh ones to replace them.

"You were kind of vague this morning when I asked what brought you to Panama. Now that I'm plying you with alcohol, can you be a little more specific?" Ken smiled, his teeth very white.

"I just needed to get away for a while," I said.

"I can see it's going to take a few more drinks before you'll talk," Ken said. We both laughed.

"I don't mean to be too mysterious," I said. "My wife died and I wanted to get away so I didn't have to think about it or talk about it."

"Oh, shit. And here I am trying to get you to talk. I'm sorry, Matt."

"No worries," I said holding up my nearly empty bottle. "Why don't you buy me another beer as an act of contrition?"

"Fair enough," Ken said, and he called for Enrique to bring us "two more of that good Jamaican beer."

We were still out on the patio when a man in a loud green Hawaiian shirt wandered out of the bar. "It's just like a couple of Americans to be sitting out in the sun when there's a perfectly good indoor bar just a few feet away," he said.

"Spoken like a true Canadian," Ken said. He introduced the man as Marty Page from Toronto. Marty was heavy set with a red face, a white goatee, and a bald head. We exchanged greetings and handshakes. "Marty is one of the few people around here who is actually retired. Everyone else works their asses off, but Marty just sits around doing nothing all day."

"I'm old and I live off the largesse of the fine people of Canada."

I must have had a quizzical look on my face because when Marty looked at me he explained, "I retired from Canada Post, the Canadian postal service."

Marty told us that several people would be arriving soon so we'd better head inside to get good seats. I followed the two men inside, but I wasn't sure what the good seats were for.

Ken, Marty and I were the only people at the bar. There was a couple at a wooden table against the wall eating nachos and drinking beer. Two men at another table across the room were engrossed in a conversation, highball glasses half-filled with ice and what looked to be whiskey. Flags from the United States, Canada, Great Britain, South Africa, Norway, and other countries I couldn't identify were hung along the walls.

The afternoon gave way to evening, and more and more people filed in. The tables and other barstools were soon full. The whole time, Enrique made sure we had fresh drinks in front of us.

"Are you boys going to have dinner?" Marty asked.

"Don't you have to head home to Lady Pamela?" Ken asked.

"I have permission to stay out to watch the game. Plus, I think she prefers it when I'm not home."

"Then let's have dinner," Ken said.

The food was served to us at the bar. Ken ordered the stir fry with rice, Marty got a hamburger so thick he had trouble biting into it, and I got fish and chips, which was served with coleslaw. Just as we were finishing our meal, a tanned man with long brown hair pulled back into a pony tail came into the restaurant. A woman with long, straight blond hair and wearing a multi-colored sun dress stood next to him. The man took off his sunglasses and waited until his eyes adjusted, then made a beeline for the bar.

"Summers, you are going down tonight," he said.

Ken turned around at the sound of his name. "Oh God, I was hoping you wouldn't show up."

"I wouldn't want to miss out on the chance to make some easy money off of you," he said. "Are we still on for a hundred?"

Ken laughed. "I'm not feeling as confident as I was last time I was here, but I'm not going to back out. I'm still in for a hundred."

"You don't have to do that, Ken," the woman said. "If you want, I'm sure Danny will let you out of the bet."

Danny gave the woman a mock look of anger, and swatted her playfully with a backhand across her upper arm. "Whose side are you on?" Danny asked.

"That's alright, Christine. I made the bet, so I'll keep it," Ken said.

Dan and Christine Longwell were originally from Fort Lauderdale, Florida but had moved to Panama five years earlier to start a small coffee farm. Dan had been a high school biology teacher back in the states, but he gave up his job and the benefits it provided to grow coffee in Panama.

"Not just coffee," he told me when we were introduced. "We produce high end, certified organic Esmeralda Especial Gesha coffee beans."

"Don't get him started talking about coffee," Christine said. "You won't be able to get him to shut up."

"Not tonight. Tonight is all about basketball," Dan said.

"What are you guys betting on?" I asked.

"The Miami Heat's playing the Lakers," Dan said. "Ken made the mistake of betting me that LA would win."

By the time the game started, I was drunk. I don't know how many beers I had, but it was plenty. At half time, Marty insisted that we all do tequila shots, which I initially refused, and then did at least three. The Heat won and Ken reluctantly handed one hundred dollars to Danny which he used to buy us more drinks. I don't remember driving back down the mountain to David, nor do I remember making my way to my room.

"You don't remember losing a beer guzzling contest to Christine or singing at the top of your lungs to 'Tainted Love,' either?" Ken asked me the next day before he left to go back to Panama City. My head was pounding and the light hurt my eyes.

"No, not any of it," I said.

"Yeah, you were a mess, but you seemed to have fun."

I didn't remember everything about the previous night, but what I did remember seemed like a good time. "Yeah, I guess I did."

"That's good. Are you still going to meet me in Panama City tomorrow night?"

I remembered telling Ken that I would meet up with him as I continued my journey south the following day. "Sure, I should be there in time to buy you dinner."

"I'll pick the place, you pick up the tab. That sounds fair."

After Ken left, I showered and started to feel a little better. It felt strange to have gone out with people I didn't know and to have enjoyed myself. For months, Lisa and I had a strained relationship, yet I rarely went anywhere or did anything without her. If I wasn't with Lisa, I was alone. I thought about the nights I sat by myself at home while she worked late, or the weekend plans that had to be canceled because she was working on a special project. I remembered how my requests for her to take time off work were met with delays and excuses. The thoughts left me cold. If Lisa was bored or unhappy with our marriage, she should have talked to me about it. She should have given us a chance to fix things—to get back to the way things were in the early days of our marriage when we were close and in love—rather than turn to someone else.

§

Ken and I met at a restaurant named Manolo Caracol in Casco Viejo, Panama City's historic district. I arrived early, so I sat at the bar and ordered a Panama Beer. I couldn't help but imagine that back at the bar in Boquete, Enrique had a smile on his face.

I was tired from my drive, but I looked forward to seeing Ken. My mind had been occupied with thoughts of Lisa—her apparent betrayal and her death—during my drive to Panama City. I was looking forward to seeing a familiar face and thinking about anything else.

"Why are you drinking that swill? Did you lose a bet?" Ken sat down on the bar stool next to mine.

"I wanted to give it a try while I was in Panama."

"What do you think?"

"It's not very good," I said, and stood up to shake Ken's hand.

"Let me buy you a decent beer."

We had a couple of drinks at the bar and made small talk before being seated for dinner. "I wanted to eat here tonight because the food is the best you can get in Panama," Ken said. "You don't order off the menu. You eat what they bring you and everything they bring you is fantastic"

I had eaten at Prix Fixe restaurants before and I normally didn't care for them. I didn't need someone I didn't know deciding what I was going to eat. But this was Ken's town, so I trusted his judgment.

The waiter freshened our drinks and then brought a lettuce salad with avocado, shredded beef jerky, and lemon herb vinaigrette. I looked at Ken, and he had a smile on his face.

"Shredded beef jerky?" I asked.

Ken laughed. "Don't be a baby. Give it a try."

I had never had beef jerky on a salad—shredded or otherwise—but I had to admit that it was pretty good. Ken waited to see my reaction after my first bite.

"See, it's not too bad, is it? Maybe you need to be a little more adventurous in your eating habits."

Lisa had said something similar about my refusal to travel outside of the country. "You need to break out of your comfort zone and experience new things," she had said. "There's so much to see and do." Look at me now, Lisa. I'm outside my comfort zone.

When we were finished with our salads, one waiter cleared our plates while another brought tall, narrow cups of pumpkin soup with cinnamon sprinkled on the top. I just shrugged and took a spoonful. It was delicious. I finished the soup, and sat back in my chair. "What made you want to move to Panama?" I asked.

I expected Ken to give me a quick, flippant answer, but instead he wiped his mouth with his napkin and seemed to be giving my question serious thought.

"I didn't think I'd ever leave California," Ken said. "I was married to a woman I loved, and my only child was off at college. Life was good. But then out of the blue one day, my wife tells me that she wants a divorce. She said she was unhappy and didn't want to be married any more. For a few months I tried to talk her out of it, then one day it hit me that if I had to beg my wife to stay married to me, maybe it wasn't in my best interest to stay married to her. So I agreed to the divorce and moved out."

Ken took a long pull on his drink, and motioned to the waiter to bring us new ones.

"I never intended to move to Panama or anywhere else. But I couldn't stand being around my ex and the home we used to share. Everything reminded me of her and I just felt like I wanted to get away. I did some research and found Panama to be affordable. At the time, I wasn't concerned about the opportunities here. I just wanted to go somewhere I could afford. So I packed up and headed here with the thought that I'd stay for a few months until I felt ready to go back to California. But after a while, Panama started feeling like home."

"Do you ever think about going back?" I asked.

"Not really. I go back to visit my son, but after a week or two, I'm itching to get back here."

The waiter set our new drinks down and then motioned to another waiter who brought the main course. "This is pork tenderloin with ancho-saril sauce," he said.

The small plate had three large slices of pork tenderloin overlapping each other with a dark sauce carefully poured over the center of the pork slices.

"It looks good," Ken said.

I cut a piece off one of the pork slices and dipped it generously into the sauce. The pork was tender and juicy, and the sauce gave it a slightly sweet cranberry taste, but with an ancho chile kick.

"Delicioso," I said.

"I didn't know you knew Spanish," Ken said.

"I don't." We both laughed.

When we had finished our entrees, the waiter brought out the dessert, which he described as naranjilla ice cream with seasonal fruits. On the plate sat two round cups; one with two scoops of ice cream and one with an assortment of fruit. The ice cream had a citrus flavor. Ken scooped up some of the fruit and then added a bit of ice cream on top of it. I followed his lead, not knowing what kind of fruit I was eating, but enjoying it all the same.

"What are your plans for after you leave Panama City?" Ken asked.

"I really don't have any. For now, at least, I plan to keep driving south. When I feel like I'm ready, I'll turn around and go home."

"That could be a problem," Ken said.

"What do you mean?"

"The road south ends not far from here, at the Darien Gap. There's no way to drive into Colombia."

"I hadn't even bothered to look at a map," I said. "I just keep following the GPS."

"You can go about another four hours south, but then the road ends. You can always fly into Colombia, but then what are you going to do for a car?"

"I guess I could sell my car here and buy another one when I get there. Do you know anyone here in Panama who buys cars?"

Ken knew someone and he introduced us the next morning. Pedro Rivera stood about five feet tall, had a round belly, and kept an unlit cigar in his mouth.

"This is a nice car," he said, "but it might be hard to sell here. Too expensive. Maybe I could ship it to Brazil where they have more money, but shipping's not cheap." He scratched his head as he stared at the car. Then he took the unlit cigar out of his mouth, motioned toward me, and made an offer to buy my Audi.

"Pedro, I told you Matt is a friend," Ken said. "You can do better than that."

Pedro looked at Ken, then at me, then back at Ken. "I could maybe do a little better," he said. He made another offer and I took it. We shook hands.

"One other thing. I'm going to need a car when I get to Medellin. Do you know anyone there?" I asked.

"No, not in Medellin. I used to know a guy in Bogota, but he died. Too bad you aren't flying to Ecuador. My brother is down there and he could help you find a car."

"Where in Ecuador?" Ken asked.

"Jorge is in Quito. He's a professor at the Central University there, but he buys and sells cars on the side. He could help you if you were going to Quito."

Ken and I looked at each other. "Is there any reason you have to re-start your trip in Colombia?"

I shrugged. "No, I can start from wherever I want."

Pedro called his brother and made a deal for me to buy a Kia Rio. It wasn't as nice as my Audi, but it would get the job done. When we got back to Ken's house, I made arrangements to fly to Quito the next day.

At dinner that night, Ken said, "You know, there's nothing that says that you have to keep driving south. You could just stay here in Panama."

The thought had occurred to me, but staying didn't feel right. I felt a primal need to keep moving, to keep heading south. I couldn't deny what I was feeling.

"That's true, but I feel a need to keep driving."

"I think I know what you mean," Ken said. "I've felt the same thing myself. But that feeling you have, I don't think you can outrun it. At least for me, the best I could do was settle somewhere and make a new life for myself. At some point, you have to stop running."

We sat in Viejo Habana, a Cuban restaurant on the corner of Avenida B and Calle 5, midway between the Plaza Bolivar and the Plaza de la Independcia, eating Cuban sandwiches and drinking Bucanero beer.

"You may be right, but I'm just not ready to stop running yet."

Ken nodded his head and then drank from his beer. "The one piece of advice I would give you is don't be afraid to talk about what you're going through. Keeping it inside can just make things worse. Let it out."

"Yeah, maybe. When I'm ready," I said.

"Sometimes you have to force yourself to be ready."

I took a bite of my sandwich and thought about what Ken had said. I knew that talking about Lisa would be painful and I wasn't ready to deal with that pain. I wasn't sure I'd ever be ready.

§

My flight into Quito arrived just after noon. Pedro's brother Jorge met me at baggage claim and then drove me in his Land Rover to a small warehouse near the university. Jorge was taller and thinner than his brother, and he dressed like a professor, not a used car dealer. Unlike Pedro, Jorge was quiet and reserved.

"I hope you like the car," he said. "If not, I have a few others."

"Okay," I said, not sure how to respond. For the first time during my trip, I felt very far from home. That shouldn't have surprised me. My car, the Audi, kept me connected to Chicago and the life I led there. Now that it was gone, I felt disconnected.

At the warehouse, Jorge pointed to a red Kia Rio. It was a four door sedan just like the Audi, but much smaller and less luxurious. The seats were cloth rather than leather and the engine was much less powerful.

"This was well taken care of," Jorge said. "It is four years old, but only has sixty-one thousand kilometers on it."

I nodded and continued walking around the car. "Can I hear it run?"

"Of course, Senor." Jorge took a key out of his pocket, got into the car, and started it. The engine turned over immediately and sounded strong. He revved the engine a couple of times and then allowed it to idle.

"Sit inside," he said as he climbed out of the car. "See if you like it."

The car was comfortable enough. The interior was clean and didn't have any unusual smells.

"Would you like to drive it?" Jorge asked.

"No, I don't think so."

"If you'd like to see the other cars, I can..."

"No, this one will do."

I paid Jorge his asking price, put my luggage in the trunk, and drove the little red car out of the warehouse. I made my way through the city to the Anahi Boutique Hotel, which Jorge had recommended. I had planned on taking a nap and going for a late dinner, but when I lay down, I couldn't sleep. So instead, I went down to the hotel restaurant, a place called Restaurant Orquideas.

I was seated at a table on the patio next to a stone fountain. The sound of the water in the fountain was relaxing, and the two glasses of Chaupi Estacia Pinot Noir that the waiter had recommended helped to relax me even more. I ordered sweet plantain ravioli with chorizo and chipotle. It sounded unusual, and after Ken's admonition the day before, I was feeling adventurous. When the waiter brought my food, I ordered another glass of wine.

The ravioli was made with wonton wrappers, which held the plantain filling. It was then covered with a spicy mixture of ground chorizo and chipotles in adobo sauce. The result was a delicious combination of sweet and spicy that had me ordering yet another glass of the pinot noir before I was finished with my meal. For dessert, I ordered one more glass of wine, and then made my way back to my room where I slept through the night.

The next morning, I drove east out of Quito until I came to E25, which I took south. I passed through Quivedo, Babahoyo, Milagro, as well as several smaller towns before I crossed into Peru near a town called Zapotillo. Somewhere along the way, the road I was on turned into the Pan-American Highway, which I took to Piura in Northern Peru where I stopped for the night.

The next day I was once again heading south on the Pan American Highway when I pulled into a service station, and the attendant, a tall, skinny kid, saw steam coming out from under my hood. He couldn't speak English, but he understood the problem. With a rag covering his hand, he removed the radiator cap, allowing more steam and water to escape. He wiped his hands on his greasy pants, and then went inside to get some water and antifreeze to refill the radiator.

"Agua," he said to me. "Mas agua."

He lugged out a large metal bucket that had a long spout for pouring, then leaned under the hood, into the engine bay, and carefully poured the water into the radiator. He emptied the bucket and poured in the coolant.

As he filled the radiator, I noticed the briny smell of salt in the air. "Are we near the ocean?" I asked. He smiled and nodded politely, then put the cap back on the radiator.

"The Pacific Ocean is just west of here," said a man with a strong accent. He must have walked up behind me when I was speaking to the attendant. I wasn't sure if he worked at the service station or if he just happened to be there.

"We must be pretty close," I said. "I can smell it." I raised my head and sniffed the breeze.

"Yes, we are not very far. Just a few miles. Have you been to Trujillo before?"

"No, this is my first time and I'm just passing through."

"You should stay, Senor, and see our pyramids."

"Your pyramids?" I asked.

"Yes, Huaca del Sol and Huaca da la Luna, the pyramids of the sun and moon. They are very famous."

I was tempted to stay to visit the pyramids, but I felt that now familiar pull to keep moving, to keep driving south. It was the middle of the day and I could still drive several more hours before dark.

"There is a tour they do from el Gran Marquez. It is very nice. You can stay there tonight and take the tour tomorrow."

I was in a mad dash to head south, but why? What was I accomplishing by speeding down the road, not taking the time to really see the countries I was driving through? I didn't have to be anywhere at any particular time. I could do whatever I wanted. "Maybe I will," I said. "What is the name of that hotel?"

With a newly refreshed radiator, I followed the directions the man at the service station gave me, and I ended up at the El Gran Marquez Hotel on Calle Diaz de Cienfuegos. It was just a few blocks off of the Pan-American Highway and very close to the Pacific Ocean.

I booked myself on the first English-speaking tour of the morning and got down to the lobby just before the bus left for the Pyramids of the Sun and Moon. The bus was modern and comfortable with large, individual seats and air conditioning. During the fifteen-minute drive to the pyramids, a beautiful woman with shimmering hair and large eyes stood up in the front of the bus and, using a microphone, told us about the history of the Huacas.

"Huaca del Sol—or Temple of the Sun—was built around 450 AD by the Moche civilization," the attractive tour guide said. She spoke English with a slight accent, and the way words fell off of her tongue, smooth and lilting, reminded me of unfolding silk. "The civilization thrived here in the Moche Valley from 100 AD to 800 AD. The Huaca del Sol was built from adobe brick, and when it was completed, contained more than 130 million bricks that were made by various communities from around the region."

Once we crossed the Moche River, we turned left off of the main highway and entered the Moche Valley. The bus stopped at a gate and then proceeded into the park to what the tour guide called the Temple of the Sun. The Pyramid was very impressive, although it had suffered a great deal of damage and wear since it was first constructed.

The tour guide wore a blue blouse with a tan skirt, the blouse pulled tight across her breasts. Her auburn hair was pulled back in a ponytail that hung down to the middle of her back. Her lips were full and she smiled brilliantly as she spoke. I felt my face flushing as sweat beaded up on my forehead.

I made myself ignore the tour guide and instead concentrated on the ruins of Huaca del Sol. I viewed the ornate carvings in the walls and the paintings that were made fifteen hundred years earlier. Who were the people who built this place? What were their lives like? Did their wives cheat on them?

"Senor, are you ready to go?"

The tour guide looked directly at me. Everyone was walking away from the Temple toward the bus while I stood there staring at a painted carving of what looked like a demon with long, sharp teeth.

"Yes, I'm sorry," I said, blushing. I turned and headed back to the bus.

We made the short drive to Huaca da la Luna, or Temple of the Moon. I tried to listen to the tour guide, but I was preoccupied with my attraction to her. It felt odd to be thinking like this after so long.

Back at the hotel, I quickly exited the bus and made my way to the restaurant where I ordered a bloody Mary. It wasn't yet noon, but I needed a drink.

I sat alone at the bar and Lisa invaded my thoughts. I wanted badly to move on with my life, to no longer feel the pain of her betrayal and death. I was tired of mourning.

The first bloody Mary went down quickly, and I ordered another. When the bartender, a young, thin man named Adelmo, set it down in front of me, he asked if I wanted to see the lunch menu. It still wasn't noon, but it was close enough. I learned from Adelmo that in Peru, lunch is the main meal of the day, which is why the lunch menu featured complete meals rather than the sandwich and fries options I was used to in the states.

I ordered a "set meal," which is three courses featuring a starter, an entrée, and a dessert at a "set" price. I chose Causa Rellena, a potato and chicken soup for my starter. The soup was thick and tasty. For my entrée, I took Adelmo's recommendation and ordered the Aji de Gallina, a chicken breast smothered in a spicy aji Amarillo sauce. I was full after the entrée, and decided to forgo the dessert. Instead, I ordered a glass of wine.

"Soon you will need a siesta," Andelmo said, placing the glass of wine in front of me.

I was stuffed and a siesta was exactly what I needed. I signed my check, and thanked Andelmo for his hospitality. When I stood, I was light-headed and felt slightly unsteady on my feet. I had to concentrate on the way back to my room, making sure not to stumble.

I lay down fully clothed on the bed and fell asleep quickly. When I awoke, the room was dark and my head was pounding. I groaned as I got up, standing too quickly and feeling dizzy. I sat back down on the edge of the bed and rubbed my temples. I stood again, this time more slowly, and made my way to the bathroom.

I splashed cold water in my face and took three aspirin. I knew from past experience that what I really needed was another drink, which would cure my headache faster than aspirin. I changed clothes and went back down to the bar.

The restaurant was busier than it had been at lunch and the bar was crowded. I was disappointed to see that Andelmo was not working. I had enjoyed his company. In his place was a large, friendly man with a fat, bearded face.

"What can I get for you?" he asked as I stood at the bar. All of the barstools were taken.

"I need a bloody Mary," I said.

"Will you be dining with us this evening?"

In my room, the idea of eating had nauseated me, but now I felt hungry, although I didn't particularly like the idea of eating at the crowded bar. "Yes. I'd like to get a table."

The bartender, who wore a name tag indicating that he was Esteban, added me to the waiting list for a table. "It should not be long," he said. "Perhaps twenty minutes."

A seat at the bar opened up next to where I was standing just as Esteban delivered my drink. I drank down half of the bloody Mary, hoping for quick relief from the pain in my head. I was not a big drinker and was not used to having a hangover, especially in the middle of the day. I tilted the drink back and finished it off.

"Did you enjoy the tour this morning?" asked a familiar, lilting voice. I turned to see the tour guide standing next to me. My stomach jumped and I felt simultaneously excited and nauseous.

"Hi," I said. "Yes, I enjoyed the tour very much.

"I'm glad. I rarely get a chance to ask people once the tour is over. My name is Laura," she said, offering her hand

"I'm Matt."

Laura's skin was soft and her grip firm. The shiny auburn hair that had been pulled back in a ponytail earlier in the day was now down and appeared to have been curled. She wore a red and white dress that hugged her hips, and white high heels.

"Would you like to sit down?" I asked, offering my barstool.

"No, thank you"

I wasn't sure what to do. She didn't want the barstool, but I didn't feel right sitting down again. I chose to lean on the barstool.

"Are you alone?" she asked.

"Yes. How about you?"

"Yes, I just wanted to get out of my apartment. I get a discount here because I work the tour, but I rarely take advantage of it. I decided to treat myself tonight." Laura's eyes were brown and incredibly clear. They sparkled as she spoke.

Esteban interrupted us. "Laura, your table is ready."

"Are you waiting for a table?" she asked me.

"I am."

"You could join me if you like." Instinctively, I wanted to beg off, to thank her for her invitation and just go back to my room, but I suddenly didn't want to be by myself.

I accepted, and the waiter led us to a table near the back of the restaurant. I was still carrying the empty bloody Mary glass, and a different waiter came to our table as we were being seated to relieve me of the empty and to take our drink order. We each ordered a glass of wine.

"What brings you to Trujillo?" Laura asked.

"I'm just passing through," I said, unsure of how to answer. "I'm heading down to Argentina." This was the first time I had ever mentioned Argentina. I wasn't really heading there. I just knew that was as far as the road went. I regretted my response, afraid Laura would ask me the purpose of my trip. Thankfully, she didn't ask.

"Are you driving?" she asked. "Did you drive from the United States?"

"Most of the way," I said. "I started in Chicago."

"Did you go through Colombia?" she asked.

"No, I cheated a little bit and flew from Panama City to Quito."

"That's too bad," she said. Colombia is a beautiful country. More modern than Peru. I am from Bogata."

"You're Colombian?" I asked. "I assumed you were from Peru."

The waiter brought our drinks and asked if we were ready to order. Neither of us had looked at our menus.

"Could you give us a couple of minutes?" I asked.

"Of course, Senor," the waiter said and walked away.

"What brought you to Peru?" I asked.

"Let's order first and then I will tell you," Laura said with a smile.

I looked over the menu, but had a hard time concentrating. Her dress was low-cut in the front and gaped open as she leaned forward, elbows on the table, studying her menu. Away from the bar, I could smell her perfume: subtle, but sexy. All of the thoughts I had tried to avoid earlier in the day came rushing back.

I had been a faithful husband. Although we never really discussed it, Lisa knew I could be trusted. Fidelity was very important to me, and I'd never considered straying. For most of the time I knew Lisa, I thought she felt the same way. Now, being here with Laura, I felt guilty being so attracted to her. I felt I was being unfaithful, but to whom?

Laura looked up and smiled when she saw me staring at her. I looked down at my menu, trying, but failing, to concentrate.

When the waiter returned, Laura ordered something called tiradito. I ordered the same thing, although I didn't know what it was.

"Would you like more wine?" The waiter asked.

"Perhaps we should get a bottle," Laura said.

I agreed. Laura said something to the waiter in Spanish. He nodded and walked away from the table.

"I ordered a bottle of my favorite Spanish wine. I hope you like it."

"I'm sure I will," I said. "You were about to tell me why you left Colombia and came to Peru."

"Oh yes. It's not much of a story. I was working as an event planner at the Sonesta Hotel in Bogata. I planned a meeting for a company that mines copper throughout South America and that's how I met my husband, Luis. I followed him back here to Peru and have been living in Trujillo ever since."

She had a husband? Why had she invited me to share a table with her? Even here in Peru, that couldn't be acceptable.

Perhaps sensing my discomfort, Laura said, "I moved to Trujillo five years ago. Luis and I were married right after I got here. He was killed three years ago in a mining accident. I keep thinking about moving back to Colombia, but I like my job with the tour company and haven't left yet.

"I'm sorry about your husband," I said, feeling inadequate.

"Thank you."

The waiter brought a bottle of wine and showed it to Laura. She said something in Spanish and the waiter poured us each a glass.

"Your tiradito will be right out," the waiter said and then walked away.

"How about you? Are you married?" Laura asked.

"Yes. Well, I was," I said, correcting myself. "My wife died in a car accident."

"I'm sorry."

I nodded. "To happier times," I said, raising my glass. We clinked glasses and each had a swallow of our wines.

"That's very good. It has a kind of spicy citrus taste," I said hoping to change the subject.

"It is a Nessa Albarino. It is one of my favorites." She turned the bottle toward me.

The waiter brought our tiradito. The dish consisted of raw fish cut in strips and placed in a piquant lime juice dressing and rocoto crème sauce.

"Have you ever had tiradito before?" Laura asked.

"No I haven't. Is it that obvious?"

Laura laughed. "You seem a little surprised."

"No, it's just…"

"It's okay. This is just like ceviche, but without the onions. I like this better." Laura took a bite and I followed suit. "What do you think?" she asked.

"I like it," I said, cutting off another bite of fish.

"I like to order this when I'm in the mood for something light."

I poured us each another glass of wine, and for the next several minutes we ate in silence.

When we finished our tiradito, the waiter came to take our plates and poured what was left of the wine into our glasses. "Would you like another bottle?" he asked.

"Yes," I said too quickly, hoping another bottle would extend our evening. My headache was gone and I was again feeling the alcohol buzz I had felt earlier in the day.

Laura smiled at my eagerness. "Now you like it as much as I do," she said.

We talked about our families and our childhoods, careful to avoid talk of our dead spouses. When we had finished our second bottle of wine, Laura suggested we each have a pisco sour.

"Have you ever had one?" she asked. I noticed a slight slur, and her accent had become more pronounced.

"No. I've never even heard of one. What is it?"

"It is the national drink of Peru." She pronounced "national" like the four syllable Spanish word nacional. "It has Peruvian pisco and lime juice and egg whites. Try it. You will like it."

We ordered pisco sours and continued our conversation. I knew I didn't need more alcohol. I was moving from buzzed to drunk, but I was enjoying my time with Laura and I didn't want it to end. The alcohol had driven away my feelings of guilt for having a pleasant time with someone other than Lisa. Why should I feel guilty? I wasn't doing anything wrong. At least I was waiting until after Lisa was dead to look for a replacement. She hadn't even waited until we were divorced.

An hour and two more pisco sours later we walked out of the bar arm-in-arm. I wasn't sure where we were going but Laura steered us toward the elevator. For a moment I thought about saying goodbye and going to my room alone, but then Laura put her arms around my neck and kissed me.

"Why not?" she asked, and I realized I'd pulled away.

"I don't know."

"We are two broken people." I could feel Laura's breath on my neck, and smell her perfume. She gently rubbed her lips on my ear, and I felt a familiar stirring inside of me. We went into my room, and locked the memory of our dead spouses out in the hall.

Laura was an eager and energetic lover. I was used to taking my time, but she wasn't interested in waiting around. How long had it been since I slept with someone other than Lisa? Laura's body felt different. It was fuller, more round in places where Lisa had been all angles. When she pulled me over so I was on top of her, I saw, for a quick moment, Lisa's eyes instead of Laura's staring up at me. Then she reached down and guided me into her, moaning softly, almost like she was humming, and all I felt was Laura. Lisa had never taken control like this, and had never been so ready. Laura's moans quickly became louder and were soon joined by my own. I panicked when I felt close to coming. What was I doing? I didn't know this woman. What if Laura had a disease or got pregnant?

I pulled out and spilled myself across her soft belly. Laura put her hand gently against the side of my head and smiled. "You have no need to worry. I cannot have babies."

Laura excused herself to use the bathroom and I lay in bed staring at the ceiling, guilt and shame creeping in. I had just met this woman and didn't know what she expected of me.

I must have fallen asleep while Laura was in the bathroom because I woke up when she slid under the covers next to me and put her hand on my chest, running it down the length of my torso.

"I want to do it again," she said, her accent strong and her words slurred.

"I'm not sure that's..."

As she began to stroke me with her hand I stopped talking and closed my eyes. Why shouldn't we enjoy each other like this? We were both single, consenting adults. There was nothing wrong with what we were doing.

Once I was ready, Laura climbed on top, controlling our movements. This time, she was less in a hurry, more patient. With her hands on my chest, she moved slowly up and down. She closed her eyes and tilted her head back, biting her lip. She leaned forward and put her face close to mine, her hair falling around my head, and softly kissed me. This went on for several minutes, Laura on top, stopping once in a while to linger, or me stopping her to prolong the inevitable. Her moans became louder and her movements more demanding, until she let out a small, high pitched yelp, her breath coming fast, and then she rolled off of me.

We lay in the bed not talking for several minutes. I wanted to say something, to make sure everything was okay, but instead stayed quiet. Laura lay with her eyes closed and a look on her face that could have been pain or ecstasy. It was hard to tell.

"That was good," she said unexpectedly, sighing with pleasure and resting her head next to mine. We fell asleep like that.

When I woke in the morning, Laura was gone. My head was pounding and I was having trouble focusing my eyes. I sat up and noticed a piece of paper lying on her side of the bed.

"Thank you for a wonderful evening," it said, and it was signed, "Laura." There was no number or email address. No way to reach her.

I felt both satiated and guilty. The sex had been great, but it shouldn't have happened. My wife had been dead for barely more than two months. What kind of man jumps into bed with another woman that soon after his wife's death? And who was I to Laura? Did she do this with every tourist she found remotely attractive? I thought back to the previous night. Even while we were in bed, I was certain I had seen pain in Laura's eyes.

My stomach rumbled fiercely. I rushed into the bathroom, and knelt in front of the toilet just in time to lose the contents of my stomach through my nose and mouth. Holding onto the sides of the bowl, I retched again, the bile burning as it came up. I stayed there on the hard tile floor for several minutes, breathing hard and spitting the vomit out of my mouth. The whole time I thought, "This is what you deserve."

When I was able, I took a quick shower, packed my things, and checked out of the hotel. I needed to get away, to leave behind what I had done.

When I got to my car, I quickly pulled out of the parking garage, but realized that I didn't know where I was going. I pulled over and took the GPS unit out of the glove box. I knew that Lima was south of Trujillo, so I punched it into the GPS and followed the directions.

A few blocks from the hotel I noticed a familiar fast food restaurant. My stomach growled and I thought it might be a good idea to get something to eat. The restaurant didn't have a drive-thru, so I went inside. As I stood in line, I thought about Laura and hoped I might run into her, but as soon as I had the thought, my guilt rose up. What would I do if I saw her? What good would it do?

§

Outside of Lima, in a town called Comas, my car started overheating again. I wanted to get mad, to blame Jorge for selling me a shitty car, but I just couldn't work up the anger. Instead, I thought back to the time I spent with Laura, and I knew that my car problems were a result of karma.

"Bullshit," I said out loud. I hadn't done anything wrong. My car was broken, but it wasn't because of anything I had done. Cars break down all the time. It was just bad luck.

I pulled over at a gas station, but no one there spoke English. Across the street was a dingy used car dealership. I picked my way through the traffic on Panamericana Norte and pulled into the parking lot.

An eight foot tall cyclone fence with razor wire on the top surrounded the lot. It looked like the type of security I would expect at a prison, not a used car dealership. I walked into the front door of a shabby building in need of paint and was greeted by a man in a dirty yellow t-shirt, sitting behind a small wooden desk.

"Do you speak English?" I asked.

The man shook his head and smiled. He was missing several teeth. He stood up from his desk and held up his hand, indicating he wanted me to wait. He went into the back of the building and when he came back out, he brought a tall, thin, balding man with him. He said something to the balding man in Spanish and then looked at me.

"Do you speak English?" I asked the balding man."

"You're bloody right I do. What can I do for you?" The balding man had a big smile.

"You're English," I said.

"And you're American."

I must have looked foolish gawking at this man the way I was, but I didn't expect to find an Englishman in the middle of Peru.

"I am. Yes, I'm an American and my car is overheating."

"Bad luck, but we can take a look at it," he said. He turned to the man with the missing teeth, said something in Spanish, and the man retreated to the back of the building.

"Diego is the best mechanic in Comas," the Englishman said. "He'll get you fixed right up."

The Englishman turned out to be Lawrence Tweed from Darlington in the north of England. He owned the used car dealership and was happy to talk to another English speaker, although he insisted that I spoke American, not English.

After I pulled my car around to the back of the building, Diego looked under the hood and Lawrence invited me in for tea. It was so stereotypical that I almost laughed when he asked.

I was surprised that among the cardboard boxes and loose papers that cluttered his office, Lawrence had a small table with two chairs and a porcelain tea set. He brought a steaming kettle from another room and poured each of us a cup of tea. "I'm afraid we're out of scones," he said. "Would you like a cracker? They may be stale." He held up an open package of Crawford Garabaldi crackers.

"No thanks. The tea will be fine."

"I'm waiting on a care package from me mum. She sends tea and scones and other goodies from home each month."

"What brought you here to Peru?" I asked.

Lawrence put his finger to his lips. "Top secret. Can't talk about it. How about you? Why are you driving around Peru with license plates from Illinois?"

"That's top secret too," I said.

"Just a couple of secretive blokes hiding out in Peru."

I laughed and took a sip of my tea. "This is very good," I said, gesturing with my cup.

"That's Yorkshire Tea," he said. "The best in the world, made by Taylors of Harrogate. You can't get that here in Peru."

I took another sip and nodded my head. "Yes, very good."

"Are you sure you don't want a cracker?"

This time, I accepted a cracker. He was right. It was stale.

Diego came into the office wiping grease off his hands with a red rag. He said something in Spanish to Lawrence and then Lawrence said to me, "Looks like you blew a head gasket, mate, but we can take care of it."

"How long do you think it will take?" I asked.

"No more than a few days. We just have to send for the part in Lima and then it won't take Diego long to swap it out."

"A few days?" I said. "Isn't there a faster way?"

"Nothing happens fast down here. The natives move to a different clock."

"What about a car? You sell cars, right? How about if I trade you my car for one on your lot?"

Lawrence's face brightened. "Now you're talking my language."

The cars on Lawrence's lot were junk. He admitted as much. Those cars were for the poor residents of Comas. He kept the nice cars—the ones meant for the wealthier residents—in a warehouse next door to his lot. He had a Mercedes and couple of BMWs and even a Ferrari in his warehouse. I settled on a two-year old Volkswagen Jetta. It was black and clean and was nicer than the Kia. Lawrence charged me too much for the car, gave me too little on my trade-in, telling me if the engine was damaged, the repair could cost more than the car was worth, and smiled the whole time he took advantage of me. I didn't care. The money from Lisa's life insurance policy—money I never anticipated having—was sitting in the bank. I might as well spend it. All I wanted was to get back on the road.

It was getting late, so I drove an hour to Lima and found a hotel just a few blocks off the main road. The next morning, I got up early and took the Panamericana Sur to Tacna, near Peru's border with Chile. I got there just past dark and felt exhausted, after sixteen hours on the road.

I stayed at the Hotel Copacabana near the airport in Tacna. It was nice enough and it was on the main road. Because I was tired, I ordered a pizza from the hotel restaurant and ate it in my room. It wasn't very good.

I had spent the day thinking about Laura and I didn't want a repeat of my time in Trujillo. No matter how hard I tried, I couldn't shake my feelings of guilt over having spent the night with her. I knew that Lisa had cheated on me—or at least I was pretty sure she had—but that didn't make it okay for me to hop into bed with a stranger, no matter how beautiful she was, less than three months after my wife's death. I expected more out of myself, and the fact that I had enjoyed the previous night in Trujillo made the guilt even worse.

The next morning, I set the GPS to Ushuaia, the southernmost city in Argentina. I had been thinking about this for some time and had decided that if I was going to keep driving south, I might as well go as far as the road would take me. There wasn't much more to my decision than that. I wanted a goal to shoot for, and Ushuaia was now my goal.

Over the next three days, I made my way along the Pacific Coast to Chile's Valparaiso Region until finally coming to Santiago. Part of me wanted to stay and explore Santiago, but I thought better of it. Since I had arrived in in the city in the middle of the afternoon, I continued driving south and got a room near Puente Alto, a large suburb south of Santiago.

The next day I made it to Victoria, where I spent the night, and then crossed through the Andes Mountains into Argentina. The temperatures had dropped considerably and I was surprised to see snow in the mountains. Thankfully, the roads were clear. When I came down out of the mountains, I took Argentina Route 181 to Route 40 into San Carlos de Bariloche.

My GPS seemed to be confused. It wanted me to swing west again into the Andes. It was getting late, and rather than get lost in the mountains, I decided to stop for the night and research my best route. I got a room at the Villa Sofia Hotel near Lake Nahuel Huapi, a large lake fed by snow melt from the Andes. The hotel was made of roughhewn logs and had rooms with high beamed ceilings reminiscent of a Swiss ski chalet.

When I checked in, the man at the front desk asked me if I was there to go skiing. When I told him I wasn't, he replied in English, "That is good because the skiing is not very good right now."

I told him about my GPS and how it was trying to send me back into the mountains.

"Yes, that is correct, Senor. The main road goes southwest into the mountains from Bariloche. There really is not much to our east." He showed me on a map how there was just open land to the east and southeast. He also showed me how I would be going across the interior of the country to the Atlantic Coast the next day after going through the mountains.

The area around the hotel was beautiful, with meticulously manicured grounds surrounded by high mountain peaks. It reminded me of a place Lisa and I had stayed when we went skiing in Aspen a year or two after we were married. The memory comforted me for a moment until her elusive behavior and phone devoid of texts took over my thoughts. I couldn't think about the good times with Lisa without also remembering the bad, so I did my best not to think about her at all.

After breakfast the next day, I was back on the road listening to music. I put on the type of loud southern rock Lisa never liked, and when I started thinking about my anger toward Lisa or my guilt over Laura, I turned up the music and sang along. Singing along to The Allman Brothers or The Marshall Tucker Band was as good a trick as any to divert my attention and keep my mind occupied.

In the late afternoon I came upon a large lake near a small town called Sarmiento. The water was choppy and the wind blew hard across it. I thought about getting out for a closer look, but I was warm and comfortable in the car, and decided to keep driving into Sarmiento to get a snack. I stopped at a restaurant called La Tranquera, which was empty except for two employees, a man and a woman.

Although neither spoke English, I was able to get my point across that I just wanted dessert. "Postre," the man said. "Si. Si." He brought me a menu in Spanish. I stared at it for a short time, and finally pointed to the Chocotorta, mostly because the word looked like "chocolate." The man nodded and went into the kitchen. A minute later he brought out a large slice of what looked to be chocolate cake with some kind of cream in the center of it. It was delicious. As I studied the cake, I could see that there was also some type of cookie or biscuit in the center that gave it a crunchy texture.

I thanked the man for his hospitality and paid my bill. He smiled and nodded a lot, but didn't say anything I could understand. I waved as I left and got back in the car.

I made it to Comodoro Rivadavia around eight o'clock that night and got a room at the Lucania Pallazo Hotel, a very nice place in the center of town. The restaurant looked welcoming, but I was still full from the chocotorta, so I went into the piano bar to get a glass of wine and relax. When I ordered a malbec from the bartender, a man two seats down from me at the bar said, "You're an American."

"I am," I said and raised my hand in a half-hearted greeting.

"Me too," he said. "From Texas. How about you?"

"Chicago."

The bartender brought my wine and the Texan scooted down to the barstool next to me. "Hank Pinkney," he said, offering his hand. He was wearing a pair of jeans with a blue and white button down shirt. His sleeves were rolled up.

I introduced myself and turned my attention to my wine.

"What brings you to Argentina?" he asked. As he did, he sat back on his barstool and I saw he was wearing a belt with a big gold buckle. I suspected he was wearing cowboy boots to complete his ensemble. I was right.

"I'm heading down to Ushuaia," I said, hoping he wouldn't ask more.

"Ah, you're going all the way south. I did that once. Do you have business down there or just going for the experience?"

"Just for the experience," I said. "I'm thinking about staying and exploring the area."

"Good idea if you have the time. I just had the weekend while I was down there. The wife wanted to go to a big music festival they put on every year."

I nodded, but didn't say anything, hoping Hank would get the message. He didn't.

"I work for Shell Oil. We have some oil fields in this area, so I spend my time going back and forth between here and Houston."

"Really?" I said, not knowing what else to say.

"Yeah, the oil fields down here are dying out though. Not much oil left any more. It wouldn't surprise me if Shell doesn't sell their leases."

Hank ordered another beer while I sipped my wine.

"Have you ever gone to Rada Tilley?" he asked.

"No, where is it?"

"Just south of here, right on the coast. It's a nice little place. They've got a real long beach, goes on for about two or three miles. The wife likes to go there whenever she comes down here with me. You should check it out."

The temperature when I'd gotten to the hotel was in the low fifties and the wind was blowing about twenty miles an hour. "Seems a little chilly for the beach," I said.

"Oh, that's true," Hank said. "Didn't think about that. I think it might warm up some next week."

I nodded and sipped the last of my wine. "Well, I'm going to head up to my room. You have a good night."

"You too. Have a good drive down to Ushuaia."

I shook Hank's hand and waved as I walked out of the bar. I wanted another glass of wine, but didn't feel sociable enough to stick around. At least I didn't take him back to my room. I laughed out loud at the thought.

The next day I made it to Rio Gallegos, where I learned from the clerk at the Hotel Patagonia that I would have to take a ferry across the Strait of Magellan to continue my journey to Ushuaia. "Just across the narrows. It is not scary," he said, detecting my fear.

"Why don't they just build a bridge?"

"Why build a bridge for when there is a perfectly good ferry?"

I put my concerns about the ferry on hold, knowing there would be time the next day to worry about it.

The restaurant at the hotel was more upscale than I wanted, so I ventured to a place called Pizza Roma Express that the front desk clerk suggested. When I got there and saw what they called pizza, I decided to get a burger.

I was nearing the end of the road. Once I got there, what was I going to do? Did it really make sense to stay in Ushuaia for any length of time? I knew nothing about the area other than it was as far south as I could get by car. This wasn't enough information to base a decision on, but it was all of the information I had.

I left the hotel early the next morning and made it to the ferry launch just a little after eight. The ferry was loading when I got there, so I pulled right onto the boat. I didn't even have to get out of my car.

The wind had died down from the previous day, and the water was relatively smooth. I was grateful for my good fortune, but still spent the short ferry ride fearing the worst.

We landed on the south side of the Straits and I pulled the car off of the ferry onto a rutted, narrow dirt road. The ferry ride had been uneventful and I felt stupid for having worried about it. I checked my GPS, turned off the dirt road onto Argentina Route 257, and began the final leg of my journey south.

§

In Ushuaia, I got a room at the Canal Beagle Hotel, a squat, square brick building that sat on the Avenue Maipu across from the commercial port. The clerk eyed me uneasily as he took my information, and seemed agitated that I had arrived without reservations. When he asked if I needed a luggage cart, I held up my single duffel bag, and shook my head. He raised an eyebrow and looked me up and down, taking in my unshaven face and stained shirt. After sending me to my room, he must have alerted hotel security.

A dark haired man in a black uniform knocked on my door and said something in Spanish. When he found out I couldn't speak his language, he introduced himself in broken English as being with hotel security. He was polite, but his questions were insistent and made me uncomfortable. Why was he interrogating me? He invited himself into my room and asked where I was from. When I told him, he tilted his head to the side like a curious dog and asked, "Chicago? In the United States?"

"Yes, that Chicago," I said.

"Ah, I see" he said, "but I checked with the airlines and they do not have a record of you flying into Argentina. How did you get to Ushuaia?" He stroked his thick black mustache and eyed me suspiciously.

"I drove."

The security man seemed incredulous. "You drove all the way from Chicago in the United States? Why would anyone drive to Ushuaia from Chicago?"

I wanted to ask him why it was any of his business, but instead I said, "I just wanted to get away for a little bit." My answer sounded more evasive than I had intended.

He eyed me and was just about to speak when I said, "I'm sorry, but why is this important to you? I can't imagine that you interrogate all of your guests."

"No, of course not," he said. "I was just curious since I have never met anyone who has driven all of the way here from the United States.

"And now you have." I walked to the door and opened it for him "I'm really rather tired after my long drive and I'd like to take a nap."

At first he didn't move or say anything. He just stared at me. Then, as if waking from a trance, he walked toward the door and said, "Of course, Senor Cravens. Please forgive my intrusion."

I closed and locked the door, then walked over to the large window that looked out at the Port of Ushuaia and across the Beagle Channel to Isla Navarino. I suddenly felt angry. "To hell with him," I said to the empty room.

§

That evening, I walked down the street toward the Canal and found a restaurant called Tia Elvira that had a big, colorful sign out front that featured a huge king crab. The place looked inviting, so I went in.

The specialty of the house was seafood, particularly crab, cod, mussels, trout, and a fish I had never heard of called hake. The seafood didn't appeal to me and they only offered two different kinds of steak, a sirloin and a tenderloin, although they offered both with a fried egg. I opted for the suprema napolitana, which, from the description, sounded like a cross between chicken cordon bleu and chicken parmesan.

It turned out to be a large chicken breast with thinly sliced ham on top, covered with mozzarella cheese and smothered in tomato sauce. It was not particularly good. The tomato sauce was bland and the chicken was mushy.

After dinner, I went into the bar for a drink. It was almost empty. I sat at one end of the bar and waited for the bartender to take my order.

"Can I help you, Sir?" the bartender asked in English.

"Do you have a beer that is made locally?" I asked.

"Yes sir, Cerveza Beagle."

I was just about to order it when he said, "It is horrible. I would not recommend it." He scrunched up his face and shook his head.

I had to laugh at his honesty. "Is there a beer you would recommend?"

"Heineken is a good beer, but you can get that anywhere. Argentina does not have good beer, but we are known for wonderful wines."

"Can you recommend one?" I asked.

"Yes, of course. I would recommend the Malbec from Bramare Marchiori Vineyards. It is spectacular."

"Then that's what I'll have," I said.

The bartender poured a small amount of wine into the glass and offered it to me to taste. I hated this part of ordering wine. Although I liked wine, I didn't know enough about it to discern the good from the not-quite-as-good. I took the wine, swirled it around in the glass and held it up to the light, then drank the sample, being sure to swish it around in my mouth before swallowing it. "Yes, this is fine," I said, saying the words I knew I would say even before I tasted the wine. The bartender poured me a glass of the Malbec and set it carefully on a white paper coaster on the bar. As he walked away I took a sip and thought about the charade I had just played. "What a fraud," I thought.

"Senor Cravens, how nice to see you again." I turned to see the security officer from the hotel standing next to me.

"Hello," I said.

"May I sit down?" he asked pointing to the barstool next to me.

"Of course," I said, immediately regretting it.

"Senor, I want to apologize for my being such poor behavior this afternoon," he said. "We have had much problems with runners of the drugs in Ushuaia recently and I am afraid I suspected you."

I nodded, neither accepting nor rejecting the apology.

"You see, I did some checking and I found out about your wife. I am sorry for your loss, Senor."

I was stunned that this security guard would check into my background like this. "How did you learn about my wife?" I asked.

"It was nothing, Senor Cravens. Just a simple check of the Internet."

"Do all security guards in Argentina do background checks on hotel guests?" My voice had an edge to it, but I didn't care. I felt like my privacy had been violated.

"Ah, I see. I am not just a security guard. I do that just part of the time to make extra money. I am a detective with the Ushuaia police. And no, I don't always check up on hotel guests. You just seemed reluctant to answer my questions, so I became curious about you. That is all."

Maybe I had acted more suspicious than necessary at the hotel. If I'd been honest with him, perhaps he wouldn't have checked up on me. And I had to admit that I looked a little rough when I first arrived. I finished the last of my wine.

"May I buy you a drink to do the apology?" he asked.

"Yes, thank you," I said.

He smiled and offered his hand. "My name is Eduardo."

I introduced myself, forgetting that he already knew my name and a lot more.

"Did you enjoy your meal tonight?" he asked.

"Honestly, no, it was not very good," I said.

Eduardo tilted his head to the side and raised his eyebrows. "What did you have?"

"Something called Suprema Napolitana."

Eduardo and the bartender, who had insinuated himself into our conversation, both shook their heads. "No, no, no. This is a restaurant of seafood. You should not order the pollo. Order the seafood. The king crab is excellent." The bartender agreed.

"I wish I would have," I said.

"Next time you will know," Eduardo said. "I wish I would have found you before the meal."

We had talked for a little over an hour when I mentioned that I would only be staying at the Canal Beagle for three days because they were going to be full with previous reservations. "Can you recommend another hotel?" I asked.

"There are many hotels," he said, "but I'm afraid they will all be full. The Festival De Musica Classica begins this weekend. Many visitors it attracts to Ushuaia."

I nodded and looked down at my drink. I wasn't sure what I was going to do, but I had a couple of days to figure it out.

"Might I make a suggestion?" Eduardo asked. "My brother owns a finca outside of town, with a guest cabin. He raises sheep. He is looking for someone to assist him on the farm. If you do not have other plans, perhaps you could keep yourself busy helping my brother and you can stay in his cabin."

I was not looking for a job nor did I have any experience working with sheep. Even so, the idea of doing some physical labor sounded good to me. I spent my life—my life before I left Chicago—sitting at a desk and thinking. Working outdoors might do me some good. I imagined myself working all day and falling into bed exhausted at night, too busy and too tired to think about my problems. Plus, it wasn't like I had anywhere else to stay in Ushuaia.

"Yes, I think that might be a good idea," I said.

"As you say in America, you can kill some birds with the stones."

§

Sebastian was a bit standoffish at first. He didn't seem as keen on the idea of having me work on his farm as his brother had been. As I learned later, Sebastian had not been looking for someone to help him, but he agreed to Eduardo's suggestion anyway. After a few days of living in the cabin and following him around his farm, Sebastian came up with the idea of having me paint his outbuildings, including the cabin. Painting kept me busy all day and relieved Sebastian of the burden of having to keep an eye on me. It worked out for both of us.

Sebastian was stout, a couple of inches shorter than my six feet, but probably thirty or forty pounds heavier. His thick gray hair and beard made him look considerably older than his brother, more like his father than his sibling. I guessed him to be in his fifties, which made him about twenty years my senior. Even so, he worked tirelessly and had enormous strength. Even on horseback, Sebastian moved like a man much younger than his age.

Sebastian's wife, Eva, was very shy. At first, she brought my dinner of locro—a navy bean and corn soup—or a stew called carbonada criolla to the cabin. She'd drop it off with very little conversation. Her English was not nearly as good as Sebastian's, and my Spanish was worse than Eva's English, so it was difficult for us to communicate. One night, Sebastian asked me to join him and Eva at the main house for a dinner of grilled lamb with chimichurri sauce. After that, I ate every night with my hosts in their home.

During one of our meals, Sebastian said, "Eduardo tells me that your wife has recently died. Is that true?"

The words of the question made it sound as if he doubted what Eduardo had told him, but the way he asked it was full of concern and sympathy. It was hard to know exactly what he was asking.

"Yes, it is true," I said. I could see in Sebastian and Eva's eyes that they had questions, but were too polite to ask. They had both been very nice to me during my stay, and although I was still not eager to talk about Lisa's death, I remembered Ken's advice when we were together in Panama City.

I told them the story about Lisa's accident, leaving out the part about our crumbling marriage. When I had finished, Eva said in broken English, "I am so sorry. Have you children?"

"No, we don't. We had planned on having kids someday. We thought we had plenty of time."

"Yes, I am sorry too," Sebastian said. He looked uncertainly at Eva and then said, "We lost our son four years ago. He had cancer. We took him all the way to Buenos Aires where they have the best doctors, but they could not save him."

Eva lowered her head and I was afraid she might be crying. There was an uncomfortable silence and then I asked, "How old was your son?"

"Tomas was seventeen when he died. He was a good boy, a beautiful boy. He was tall and was a wonderful soccer player. He was on the junior team in Ushuaia." Then softly, Sebastian said, "He was our only child."

Eva got up from the table and took a framed photo off of a shelf and handed it to me. "This is Tomas," she said. "He would be twenty-one now."

I was relieved to see that Eva was not crying. I took the photo from her. Tomas was tall and thin in his blue and white soccer uniform. He had curly black hair and an awkward smile. "He's a good looking kid," I said.

"Yes he was," Eva said. She took the photo from me and returned it to the shelf.

The room was quiet until Eva returned to the table and Sebastian asked, "Do you know how long you will be staying?"

"I'm not sure," I said. "I don't feel like I'm ready to go back home yet, but if you need me out of the cabin, I can always try to find a hotel room in town."

"No, no. You do not have to leave," Sebastian said, his voice full of apology. "You can stay as long as you like. We enjoy having you here and you are very helpful painting the buildings and helping with the sheep."

"Thank you," I said. "That's very kind." I was pleased that I would not have to hunt for an open hotel room and relieved that I would not have to return to Chicago. At least not yet.

§

I was up on a ladder painting the side of the barn when I heard Sebastian call me from inside the shearing shed. When I got there I saw that one side of the interior sheep pen had collapsed and Sebastian had his hands full trying to prop it up. The dozen or so sheep that were in the pen clamored over each other to get out all at once.

The pen was set up in the corner of the barn and the square enclosure consisted of the side and back wall of the barn on two sides and green metal gates on the other two sides. The gates on the front of the pen had come loose from the floor, and the weight of the sheep against them had pushed them forward. Sebastian held the gates up as best he could, but the combined weight of the sheep made it difficult for him.

"What can I do?" I asked Sebastian.

"Come hold this right here so I can put the posts back into the floor."

As I held the gates in place, Sebastian took two L-shaped metal rods off the wall where they were hanging on a nail, slipped them through collars on the two center gates, and pushed the rods down into holes in the concrete floor. The rods anchored the gates at the center of the pen, holding them upright and allowing me to let go.

"Thank you, my friend," Sebastian said. "I must have forgotten to replace the support rods yesterday when I took the pen apart to clean."

I had never been in the shearing shed before and I was surprised at how neat and organized it was. In the back left corner was the pen that had collapsed on Sebastian. The floor in the pen was made of concrete and was very clean. There was a sliding door at the back of the barn that allowed sheep to come in from outside, and the gates at the front of the pen opened into the shearing pen, which had an even more spotless concrete floor and two cords hanging from the ceiling. At the end of one cord was a toggle-type switch and on the other were electric shears, which resembled a large hair trimmer.

As I watched, Sebastian led a sheep into the shearing pen. He sat the sheep down on its hind legs and then gently flipped it up so that none of its feet were on the ground. When he did this, the sheep became very still and did not fight against him or try to get away. Sebastian then expertly sheared the sheep, first cutting carefully around the animal's crotch, and then starting under the chin, he ran the shears down to the bald spot he had created initially, and proceeded to shear the rest of the sheep in just a few minutes. When he was done there was a large, one-piece wool fleece on the floor along with a few smaller pieces.

Sebastian released the sheep into a pen opposite the holding pen. At the rear of the second holding pen was a door that was open to the outside. As Sebastian closed the gate to the second holding pen, the sheep scampered out of the barn into the pasture. Sebastian tossed the fleece into a square metal container, then led another sheep from the first holding pen into the shearing pen, repeating the process.

I sat on an upturned plastic bucket as Sebastian sheared one sheep after another. "You are very good at that," I said.

Sebastian laughed at my comment. "You can get good at anything if you do it long enough," he said, and then added, "except perhaps marriage."

"That's sad, but true."

"I'm not sure if we ever get truly good at marriage. Eva and I have been married for twenty-six years, but I'm still trying to figure out how we can live together and be happy."

I was a little surprised at Sebastian's comment. He and Eva seemed very happy together. In fact, often when I watched them, I wished that Lisa and I could have been as close.

"For Lisa and me, it seemed like our earliest days were our happiest. The longer we were married, the further apart we became." The words were out of my mouth before I even realized I was saying them.

"It is that way sometimes," Sebastian said.

I had the urge to talk, to unburden myself of all of the thoughts and feelings I was keeping locked up inside. We were quiet for several moments and I thought again about the conversation I had with Ken when I visited him in Panama City. I wasn't sure if I was ready to talk about Lisa, but, like Ken said, sometimes you have to force yourself to be ready.

"Before Lisa died, she was acting very strange. She seemed to be avoiding me, spending extra time at her job and leaving the room when I would come in. Something was going on with her, but I'm not sure what it was."

Sebastian nodded his head as he listened. "Did you ask her about it?

"Not at first, but after it had gone on for a few months, I confronted her. I told her it was obvious something was wrong. At first, she denied it, just said she was busy or I was imagining things, but one day she promised that she would tell me what was going on when she got home from work. That was the day she died in the car accident. I still don't know for sure what was going on with her, although I have my suspicions.

"What do you think was wrong?"

"I think she was seeing someone else and she was going to tell me she wanted a divorce." Hearing the words come out of my mouth was painful, but it was also a relief to get them out in the open.

Sebastian was no longer shearing sheep. He had stopped and was listening to me talk. He glanced down at his hands, rubbing them together like he was trying to warm them up. "Does it really matter?" he asked, shrugging. "I don't mean did it matter before. I mean, does it matter now? Now that Lisa is gone."

I was about to say, "Yeah, it matters," but instead I took a moment to think about Sebastian's question. It hurt me to think that Lisa was seeing someone else, but how important was it now? If she was having an affair, it was over. Lisa was dead. We may have had problems, but when Lisa died, she was still my wife.

“I’m not sure how important it is anymore.”

“My son was a good boy, but he could also be bad. When he was going through treatments in Buenos Aries, Eva and I found some drugs—marijuana and some pills—in his bedroom. We also think that he and his friends stole a car in town. I don’t mean to compare these things to what you have said. It’s just, when Tomas died, none of those other things mattered. I wasn’t angry with him. I wasn’t disappointed in him. I just loved him and my love was too strong, too consumidor—I don’t know the English word—but I couldn’t feel any anger or disappointment.”

I understood what Sebastian was saying. “You think I’m focusing on the wrong thing?”

“I know that the love can make you stronger and can get you through your tough times. Anger makes you weaker. It wouldn’t have done any good for me to be angry at Tomas. It wouldn’t have changed things. So I just felt the love I had for my son.”

§

My time was running out in Ushuaia. I had finished painting all of the buildings on Sebastian’s farm, and I knew that my brother could only cover for me for so long.

“I’m sorry, Matt, but Greg wants to meet with you a week from tomorrow,” Scott said when I called him the night I finished with the painting. “I had promised myself that I wouldn’t pressure you to come back before you were ready, but we really need the Conover contract.”

Scott had been incredibly supportive, and although I didn’t want to go back yet, I knew that I had to. The survival of our company depended on keeping Greg Conover as a client. We had worked too long and too hard to build the company. I couldn’t allow my lingering feelings of grief and betrayal to get in the way of our continued success. “I just need to make the arrangements and then I’ll be home,” I told him.

At dinner that night, we celebrated the painting of the buildings. Eva made cumin pork with sweet potato guiso, one of Sebastian's favorites. I was glad that I had finished the painting before leaving. I was also happy that Sebastian was pleased with my work.

"The buildings are beautiful," Sebastian said as we sat down to dinner. "I am proud to own them."

When we had finished the meal and Eva was going around re-filling our wine glasses, I told them that I had some news. Eva stood behind Sebastian's chair and they both had concerned looks on their faces. I was sure that they knew what I was about to say.

"I spoke to my brother earlier," I said. "There is a meeting soon with a very important client, and I need to be there for it. As soon as I can make arrangements, I'm going to be leaving to go back to Chicago."

"Are you sure?" Eva asked. "You are welcome to stay longer."

"Yes, stay longer if you wish," Sebastian said.

"Thank you. You've both been wonderful hosts, but I think it's time for me to go home and get on with my life."

I heard the words come out of my mouth, but I wasn't sure that I completely believed them.

§

The closer Sebastian and I got to Rio Grande, the more traffic we encountered. We left the narrow, mud-covered roads behind us and traded them for wider roads surrounded by homes and businesses. Once in the city, traffic came to a standstill as tourists stopped and snapped pictures of a giant sculpture of a sea trout, its head angled up in the air and its tail the size of an automobile. Banners along the roadway announced Rio Grande as the "International Fly Fishing Capital of the World," a rather audacious claim from a city that looked so worn and dusty.

"I don't know how people live in such a place," Sebastian said. "So much noise and traffic. How do you say, it drives me buggers."

I laughed. "The traffic here reminds me of Chicago, just on a smaller scale."

"And you want to go home to that? You should stay with us."

I didn't respond. What if I didn't go back to Chicago? What if I returned to the Finca with Sebastian? It was a foolish thought, and the answer didn't matter. I was heading home whether I liked it or not.

"I'm going to pull over here to get fuel. Do you want to eat?" Sebastian asked.

We had eaten breakfast—medialunas, a small, sweet croissant, with butter—before we left Sebastian's farm, but I was starting to get hungry. "Sure, I can eat something."

"You are like me," Sebastian said, laughing. "You can always eat something. I know a good restaurant in town. They have very good pizza. It is my favorite. You probably cannot get good pizza in Chicago, so you should have some before you leave Argentina."

Sebastian seemed so pleased to be sharing his favorite pizza with me that I couldn't bring myself to tell him about how Chicago was known for its pizza.

We drove into downtown Rio Grande and parked in angled parking on Perito Moreno Street across from a pizzeria named Don Peppone. The restaurant had a large red and green sign that featured a character that looked like a younger version of Chef Boyardee twirling his moustache. As we walked across the street, cars honked their horns and one man shouted at us in Spanish, but Sebastian was unconcerned. The smell of garlic, sausage, and rising dough was in the air, and, like a bloodhound, he was locked onto the scent.

Inside the restaurant, we were seated at a small wooden table. The waiter came and Sebastian ordered a pepperoni pie for both of us, and a Cerveza Quilmes for himself. I ordered a Diet Coke, my first since arriving in Tierra del Fuego. The pizza had a very thin crust and was covered in pepperoni and tomato slices, but lacking cheese. Sebastian spoke glowingly of the pizza, saying it was the best in Argentina. I agreed that it was the best I had eaten during my time in the country.

"Have you eaten pizza anywhere else in Argentina?" Sebastian asked.

"No, so this is the best I have had, and also the worst," I said.

Sebastian gestured with his hand as if to dismiss me. He let out a deep laugh and grabbed another slice. He was clearly enjoying the experience.

§

After lunch, Sebastian and I were back on the road heading north out of Rio Grande. The rain let up as we drove along the road that ran parallel to the sea. "That is my bay," Sebastian said smiling. "It is named after me."

"That's the Bay of the Old Sheep Herder?" I asked.

Sebastian let out a guttural laugh I had come to appreciate. "A sense of humor can be a dangerous thing, my friend. Especially for a gringo," he said, wagging his finger at me and smiling. "That is the Bay of San Sebastian."

The water of the Bay seemed impossibly blue, a deep cobalt, and stood in sharp contrast to the muted brown of the land. The water was tranquil. As we drove, I looked out at it and felt myself relax. The feeling was short lived. When the road turned inland and we moved away from the water out onto the expansive brown plain, I lost the calm feeling and started thinking too much about the drive, and the flight home, and getting back to work, and about Laura, and of course, about Lisa. Roads branched off in all directions. I never saw any road signs, but Sebastian drove with the confidence of a native who had traveled this way many times. More than once I asked, "Do you know where you're going?"

"Of course," came the reply. "Relax, my friend, and enjoy the view."

We drove in silence for a few minutes before Sebastian said, "Are you sure you want to go home? I could find you more work to do."

I stared out the window at the flat, brown plain. Returning to Sebastian's finca was enticing. It was safe and quiet and most of all, when I was there, I wasn't surrounded by all of the things that reminded me of Lisa. Even so, it was time to stop running away from my problems and face them head on. Returning to my home and my job and my life wouldn't be easy, but it was necessary. I couldn't hide at Sebastian's forever.

"I have to go home sometime," I said to Sebastian. "I guess now is as good a time as any."

Sebastian did not look at me, but simply nodded his head and continued to drive.

§

At times, it seemed we had the road to ourselves. We seldom saw any other vehicles. But as we got closer to the ferry launch, we began encountering more semi-trucks. There were often three or four of them running together. When we approached the trucks from the rear, Sebastian easily passed them. There were no lines painted on the road, so it was difficult to tell if we were in a passing zone or not. Sebastian didn't seem to care one way or the other.

Although the airport was in Rio Gallegos, which is in Argentina, we had to cross into Chile to get there, the border between the two countries separated by the Strait of Magellan.

"How much longer to the ferry?" I asked.

"Not much longer," Sebastian's said.

"I'm going to miss Eva's cooking," I said, just to have something to say.

Sebastian nodded.

"Now with my experience, maybe I can get a job as a painter."

"Or a sheep shearer."

We both laughed. I tried to think of something else to say, but couldn't come up with anything, so we rode in silence.

Sebastian slowed and then turned onto the same unmarked, rutted dirt road I had taken when I got off the ferry on my way to Ushuaia. Unlike the Bay of San Sebastian, the water of the Strait of Magellan was gray and roiling, with whitecaps that made me uncomfortable. "This is where we will meet the ferry," Sebastian said. "We are first in line."

"The water is really rough," I said.

"Yes, but it will be fine," Sebastian said, an air of certainty in his voice. His confidence didn't assuage my fears.

We had only waited a few minutes when two large Scania semi-trucks pulled in behind us. They were both blue and each carried a cargo container. The drivers got out, waved at us, and then stood next to their trucks smoking and gesturing with their hands as they spoke. Sebastian pointed to a sign nailed to a wooden post off to the side of the road. It said that the ferry would be back in about twenty minutes.

Conversation with Sebastian suddenly felt strained. I think we both understood that once we boarded the ferry and made our way across the water, we'd soon be at the airport and then I would be gone. So we talked about the weather, about Eva's cooking, and about a large sheep farm we had seen earlier in our trip. The discussion was forced and I felt bad that after all of the wonderful conversations Sebastian and I had shared, we were now unable to talk to each other easily and naturally.

A few minutes later another Scania truck pulled into the line.

"Here comes the ferry now," Sebastian said.

In the distance, against the white-capped waves, the ferry seemed insubstantial. As it drew closer, I saw that it carried only one truck from the other side.

The ferry pulled right up to the shore at the end of the road and lowered a ramp from the end of the boat. It reminded me of landing crafts I had seen in films of the D-Day invasion at Normandy. I was hopeful that our journey across the Strait would be less eventful than what I had seen in those films.

The truck that was on the ferry pulled off and drove away up the dirt road. We were then waved onto the boat followed by the three Scania trucks. Although we fit on the ferry, I was concerned about the weight.

Sebastian must have sensed my unease. "It will be fine," he said once again, and then pointed out at the water. "This is called the First Narrows. It is the narrowest part of the Straits. We'll be in Patagonia soon." I smiled and nodded, my stomach continuing to twist into knots.

As the ferry pulled away from shore, I thought about my journey home. Was I really ready to go back to Chicago to face life without Lisa? Truthfully, I wasn't sure, but there was only one way to find out. I knew I would likely never make my way to Ushuaia again. It wasn't the kind of place you stopped on your way to somewhere else. In fact, being at the end of the road, it wasn't on the way to somewhere else.

Maybe whatever was going on with Lisa in those weeks and months before her accident didn't matter anymore. Maybe what mattered was that she had been my wife, and that at least for a while, we had loved each other.

Although he stood right next to me, I was already starting to miss Sebastian. He had become a good friend. Even so, I knew that my future was back in Chicago, not here in Tierra del Fuego, and not at Sebastian's finca. This place had been a refuge at a time I needed to hide, but Chicago was still home.

"Next stop, Rio Gallegos," Sebastian said smiling.

I nodded, and stared across the roiling water toward the horizon on the other side.

Lake of the Falls

We rode in silence, making our way through the Chicago morning traffic. Dad spent most of his time quietly looking out the passenger-side window.

"What kind of car is this?" he asked.

"It's a BMW 750LI," I said.

"It's nice," he said, without much enthusiasm, then resumed his watch out the side window. I could feel where this conversation was heading, and I didn't like it. I had spent most of my life having some variation of this discussion with my dad, and I figured the best thing to do was just be quiet. A few more minutes passed in silence, then Dad asked, "So how much did it cost?"

He couldn't simply say that the car was nice. He had to know how much I paid for it. And the thing was, I didn't mind telling him, but I knew where the conversation was going to go from there.

"How much did what cost?" I asked.

"The car. How much was the car?"

"I don't remember," I said.

"How long have you had it?"

The conversation made me feel like I was going down a long, steep slide, and I couldn't stop myself. "About a year," I said.

"You bought the car a year ago and you can't remember how much you paid for it?" Dad asked, his voice rising in volume and incredulity.

"I don't remember exactly," I said. "There was a trade-in, and I bought some extra stuff."

Dad turned away from the window and glowered at me, gesticulating with his hands.

"Give me a ball park. What did the car cost in round numbers? I'm just curious."

"I don't know," I said. "It was around eighty-five thousand dollars." I coughed as I said the number.

"I'm sorry, how much?"

"Eighty-five thousand dollars," I said again, this time without the cough.

"Are you serious? That's more than three times what your mother and I paid for our house." Dad based the value of just about everything on how it compared to what it had cost him to buy our home in Mercer, Wisconsin.

"Yeah, I know, Dad. But that was a long time ago."

"It was thirty-four years ago, and now you're paying three times as much for a car."

"That's my point exactly," I said. "Today you could sell your place for ten times what you paid for it."

Dad slumped in his seat and turned glumly toward the window again. "Is that what you think I should do? Sell the land?" We'd had this conversation before.

"Dad, I don't care if you sell the land. That's up to you. I'm just saying, you bought that property a long time ago and I bought my car last year. Things have changed."

"You're not kidding they've changed. Eighty-five thousand dollars for a car? Don't they make cars for less than that?"

"Of course, but I like this one and I can afford it. What's wrong with buying something nice?"

"There's nothing *wrong* with it," he said. "It's just not necessary. You drive from your house to the parking lot at work and you leave it in the parking lot while you work sixteen hours every day. Then you drive back home, park the car again, and leave it there while you sleep. Why do you need an expensive car to do that?"

As an attorney, I had to be concerned with entertaining clients, tax write-offs, and keeping up appearances. Dad had worked for the state as a forest ranger when I was young, and he didn't have to think about such things. His car was just a conveyance from point A to point B.

"I don't work sixteen hours every day, Dad. Once in a while it's necessary, but most days I'm only in the office for ten or twelve hours." The words were out of my mouth before I could stop myself.

"Twelve hours? You only spend half your life working. So you have plenty of time to enjoy your expensive car."

"What difference does it make how much I spend on a car?"

"It's not just the car, Kevin. It's the way you live."

My relationship with my dad had been contentious ever since he moved our family to Mercer. We had been living in Aurora, about forty miles southwest of Chicago, and, as far as I was concerned, we were happy. I was twelve years old, and had a group of friends that I enjoyed. I didn't want to leave Aurora, but Dad never asked my opinion. We had sparred with each other ever since.

"You're exaggerating, Dad. If I don't work all those hours, someone else will, and I'll be out on the street. If I had chosen to do something else with my life, things might be different. But if I want to do well at the law firm, I have to keep working."

"You're a partner. Shouldn't you get more time off?"

I looked out the side window and let out a brittle laugh. We were leaving Illinois and crossing into Wisconsin. "Just the opposite," I said. "I'm expected to be there and lead by example. The clients expect more out of me because they're paying more to have me involved in their cases, and the firm expects more because I'm making more money."

Dad was silent for a long time before he said, "I just think you should spend your time enjoying your life instead of spending it to make money."

"I know, Dad, but..." Dad looked at me, waiting to hear what I had to say. I wanted to argue, but what could I tell him? That my partners would miss me if I spent my time enjoying my life? They wouldn't miss me. They would just replace me and move on.

What about my friends? That one hurt. I didn't really have any. I had lost touch with my friends from high school and college. I was always too busy to visit them or meet with them when they came to Chicago. My replies to their emails were always short with promises of writing again when I had more time. I never had more time, so my promises were never kept. I'd occasionally have dinner or stop for a drink with some of the lawyers from my firm, but we were work acquaintances.

"Just forget it," I said. "I don't want to fight."

Dad turned to look out the window again, and we rode in silence.

§

The further north we traveled, the more energy Dad seemed to have. Near Portage we followed I-39 north and pulled off the Interstate at Coloma to eat lunch at an A&W on Highway 21. Dad ordered a cheeseburger and promptly devoured it. I had a chili cheese dog, the first I'd had in many years.

Dad sipped his root beer. "Whatever happened with you and Becky?"

Dad was the only person in the world who called my ex-wife, Rebecca, Becky. We had been divorced for nearly eight years.

"What do you mean?" I asked. "You know what happened."

"Sure, but why did you get divorced?"

"I don't know, Dad. Sometimes marriages just don't work out."

Rebecca had been an assistant curator at the Museum of Contemporary Art in Chicago when I met her. We were in our late twenties and we were both desperate to establish our careers. Rebecca was smart and funny and beautiful. She was everything I wanted in a wife. After dating for almost two years, we were married and bought a house in Chicago's upscale Lincoln Park neighborhood, just a few blocks from Lake Michigan.

At first, our life together was fun and exciting. We'd work hard during the week, play hard on the weekends, and every couple of months we'd head up to Mercer to see my mom and dad. It was actually more Rebecca's idea to visit my parents than it was mine. When I left Mercer, I wanted to get away from the small town, the isolation, and perhaps most of all, my dad. But Rebecca loved my parents and missed them if she didn't see them every couple of months.

My parents returned Rebecca's love. Mom took her blueberry picking, and they'd sit for hours down on the dock just talking. Dad teased her about being afraid to take a fish off the hook, and showed her off to his friends when we went into town. Rebecca brought something out in my dad that I hadn't seen from him while I was growing up.

A couple of years into our marriage, I started working more hours, and spent most of my weekends at the office. Rebecca tried to be understanding, but she didn't get married just to spend her time alone in an empty house. She'd plan special dinners or weekend getaways, but, more often than not, I cancelled them because I was so busy making a name for myself at the office. Even if we did get away for the weekend, I spent most of my time doing work.

When Rebecca started talking about having kids, I tried to avoid the conversation. I was pushing hard at work to become a partner, and I really didn't have time for kids. I told her that we could start a family after I became a partner.

This went on for years until Rebecca finally insisted that we visit a marriage counselor. I fought the idea at first. Marriage counselors were for couples involved in abusive relationships plagued by alcohol or drug abuse. They weren't for "normal" people who just worked hard. At least that's what I thought. Rebecca thought differently and eventually won the argument.

I went through the motions, but my heart just wasn't in the counseling sessions. It's not that I didn't want our marriage to work out. I did. But working out to me meant maintaining the status quo. I wanted to be able to work as many hours as I needed to work, and I didn't want my wife to complain.

When it became obvious that I wasn't going to change, Rebecca said she wanted a divorce.

"You want a divorce because I work hard?" I asked. "Who criticizes her husband for being a good provider?"

"You know that's not what I'm doing," she said. "I just want some balance."

"What balance? Everyone I know works as many hours as I do. You expect me to turn my back on all the hard work I've put into my career so I can be home with you?"

I wasn't trying to save our marriage. I was trying to win an argument. It was the last gasp effort of a desperate man. I knew Rebecca was right, but I couldn't make myself give in. I wasn't willing to give up all of the hard work I had put in at the office. The damage had been done. If Rebecca wanted a divorce, then I would give her a divorce. It was a horrible mistake.

"Well, it's too bad," Dad said. "I really liked Becky."

"Yeah," I said. "Me too."

§

As we drove across Lake Dubay near Stevens Point, I noticed the leaves were changing, painting the lakeshore with an autumnal brush. Dad was wide-eyed.

"You know, your mom loved this time of year," he said. "She loved the cooler weather and the changing colors." Dad swept his hand across in front of him, indicating the colorful fall foliage.

"I was always more of a summer guy," I said. "I loved the heat and being out on the water."

"I know you did. That's why I always figured you'd move back to Mercer after law school."

"You did?" I asked.

"Well, yeah," he said. "I mean, your mom and I were there, and I just thought you loved it up in the Northwoods."

I was surprised Dad didn't realize that I never had any intention of going back to Mercer. In fact, I was running away as fast as I could. Dad also didn't seem to understand that he was the main reason I didn't want to go back.

"I don't know," I said. "I guess it was just time to grow up."

Dad gave me a quizzical look.

Our house in Mercer was cramped. There was only one bedroom, which meant I had to sleep on a bed tucked into the corner of the living room. I had no privacy. Late on our second night in the house, I was having trouble sleeping. I heard Mom and Dad talking in their room. They weren't yelling, but I could tell by their tone that they were having an argument. I couldn't make out everything that was being said, but what I could make out infuriated me. Dad had had an affair, and moving to Mercer was the result.

I talked to my mom the day after I overheard her conversation with Dad. I didn't want to let on that I had been listening to them, but I needed to let her know how unhappy I was.

"This isn't fair," I said. "I don't want to live here. This isn't even a house. It's a shack. And there are no kids up here. This is all Dad's fault, and it's not fair to you or me."

Mom was sympathetic, but she wasn't going to talk against Dad. "You're going to grow to love it up here, Kevin. There's so much to do. You can swim and fish and hike. And I'm sure there are kids your age up here. You just haven't met them yet. Your dad is going to fix up this house and you'll learn to love it just like we do."

Mom's devotion surprised me. Even years later, on her deathbed, she asked me, "Are you still angry at your father for moving us to Mercer?"

At that point, I was forty-three years old and Mom knew that I still held a grudge against Dad. "No, Mom," I lied. "That was a long time ago."

"Just remember," she said, "he did what he thought was best."

Best for him, I thought, but didn't say anything.

§

In Tomahawk, the four-lane Interstate gave way to two-lane U.S. Route 51, the main north-south artery of Northern Wisconsin. It was the road we were on when I first saw Mercer as a boy.

Sitting in the back seat of our station wagon, I had become more and more embittered with each mile we traveled. It didn't matter to me what Mercer was like. I had my mind made up that I was going to hate it.

As we approached town, Mom said, "There's the water tower. We're here. We're in Mercer." Dad's face became animated. I looked around, but all I saw were trees.

"There's nothing here," I said.

"Just wait a second. The town's right up the road," Dad said.

As we entered Mercer, I saw a grocery store and a motel. There was an old brick building on the corner and some sort of store with a big wooden Indian across the street. There were a few more storefronts along Route 51 and then it was back to more trees.

"That was it? That was the whole town?" I asked.

We drove north on Route 51 for another mile or two then turned left onto County Road FF. It was one of the windiest roads I had ever been on. After a while, Dad turned off the blacktop and onto a dirt road that wound through the woods. There were narrow white signs in the shape of arrows nailed to the trees. The signs had names on them, but I didn't see our name.

We pulled off of the dirt road onto an even narrower dirt path. As it turned out, that was our driveway. We drove through the trees up to a small house that was in bad need of paint. It had been white at one time. There was no garage and no yard.

"Welcome home," my mom said. I felt like I was going to get sick.

The house sat on twenty-five acres of woods and we had two hundred feet of frontage on Crystal Lake. What we lacked in grass, we more than made up in pine, maple, hemlock, and birch trees.

Over time, Dad fixed up the house and built an addition, including a bedroom for me. He converted what had once been a shack into a comfortable home. He also added a two car garage and attached a basketball hoop above the pull-down door.

Mom never seemed to hold a grudge against Dad. She was always loving toward him, and attentive to his needs. I don't remember a time when she wasn't supportive of him. She was certainly more forgiving than me.

§

Driving into Minocqua, Dad and I both marveled at how much the town had grown. Both sides of the road were lined with stores and restaurants and real estate offices. Traffic was heavy for an off-season Thursday afternoon.

We drove across Lake Minocqua and I remembered my first water skiing tournament. Just as I was about to say something about it, Dad said, "It was right down there that we took you to your first water skiing tournament. You hadn't been skiing for very long, but you still finished fifth out of seventeen skiers in your age bracket. Do you remember that?"

I was stunned. "Yeah, I remember. I'm surprised you do."

"Oh, I remember. We went down to Bosacki's Boathouse afterwards to celebrate. Your mom and I were both proud of you, but all you could talk about was how you should have done better."

"I don't remember that." We were driving past Paul Bunyan's Cook Shanty, a Minocqua landmark. The giant statue of Paul Bunyan and his blue ox, Babe, stood next to the restaurant sign near the road.

"You're never satisfied, Kevin. You always want more." Dad had turned in his seat to face me.

"That's not true," I said. "I'm satisfied with what I have."

"Is that why you work so many hours at your job? Or why you have to have such an expensive car? Trust me, Kevin, I know how you feel. I used to be that way myself. I always wanted more. That was one of the reasons your mom and I decided to move to Mercer."

I pulled up to the stop light at State Route 70 and impatiently rubbed my hands on the steering wheel. I found Dad's explanation of why we had moved to Mercer irritating. "I've never heard that."

"Never heard what? That I used to be like you or that one of the reasons we moved to Mercer was to get out of the rat race?"

"Both. I've never thought of you as someone who was very ambitious. I don't remember you ever talking about things you wanted to buy or plans you had for the future." My cheeks began to burn.

"It's not really a matter of being ambitious," he said, apparently not taking offense to my statement. "My focus was always on what I lacked, not what I had."

That was news to me. I had never known my dad to strive for more in life. In fact, I had always considered him a bit of a failure. We lived in a small house in the middle of nowhere, he and Mom drove old cars, and it always struck me as odd that Dad was perfectly happy living that kind of lifestyle. He never wanted to improve himself or do better in life.

"I didn't know that," I said. The light turned green and we continued north on Route 51.

"There's a lot you don't know." Dad said, turning his attention to the buildings as they drifted by.

§

The landmarks became more familiar as we approached Mercer. We passed Little Bohemia, where John Dillinger once hid out and got into a gun fight with the FBI, then the Manitowish Waters Airport. We crossed

County Road W that went down to LaPorte's IGA grocery store and the Rest Lake ski bowl, where I used to ski with the Manitowish Waters Skiing Skeeters. A few moments later, we were in Iron County.

Dad smiled when we came to State Route 47 and he saw the Ding-A-Ling Supper Club. The Ding-A-Ling had been Mom and Dad's favorite place to eat.

"We had some good meals in there," Dad said, smiling.

As soon as the Mercer water tower came into view over the trees, Dad said, "There it is," as if he had just seen the Taj Mahal. "What do you want to do first?" Dad asked.

"I thought we should probably go check into the hotel and maybe you can take a quick nap before we go out for dinner."

"I don't need a nap," Dad said, waving his hand dismissively. "Let's go have a drink at the Heart."

"I thought you quit drinking," I said.

"I haven't had a drink in three years, but that doesn't mean that I quit."

We both laughed. "All right, let's go to The Heart."

When I was in high school, Dad used to go to The Heart of the North bar after my basketball games. It was a ritual with him. He'd drop Mom and me off at the house and then head back into town. Mom was always happy to let him go, which I thought was odd. I couldn't understand how trusting she was of him, and I resented the fact that he decided to go drinking instead of spending time with us.

When we walked into The Heart, Dad stopped inside the door and looked around. Everything was just as I remembered it. We walked to the bar and sat down.

"Can I help you fellas?" the bartender asked.

"Two Leinies," Dad said, ordering for both of us.

The bartender brought the beers.

"Boy, this place hasn't changed much," Dad said.

"No, I suppose not," the bartender said, laughing. "So you've been here before?"

"We used to live up here," Dad said. "Does Frank Althaus still own the bar?"

"I'm afraid not," the bartender said. "Frank had a heart attack a little over a year ago. After he died, I bought the place from Mrs. Althaus."

"Frank is dead?" Dad said. "I hadn't heard."

"I'm Charlie Payne," the bartender said, extending his hand.

"I'm Stan Hargrove," Dad said. "And this is my son, Kevin."

We shook hands.

"Hargrove? Are you the Hargrove that used to be the forest ranger?"

"That's me," Dad said.

"Then you must be the famous basketball player," Charlie said to me.

"I played basketball," I said, laughing. "But I'm not famous."

"Oh, you are. Look at this," Charlie said. He walked over to the wall next to the bar, took down a framed photo, and brought it over to us. "Mrs. Althaus told me all about this picture when I bought the bar." It was a photo of me in my high school basketball uniform taking a jump shot. "She said it was one of Frank's favorite pictures and that he was good friends with your dad."

"That was a game against Hurley during Kevin's senior year," Dad said. "Hurley had a 15 point lead, but Mercer came back in the fourth quarter. That shot by Kevin tied the game and sent it into overtime. Mercer ended up winning the game, and Kevin scored twenty of the team's final twenty-five points."

"No wonder Frank liked that picture so much," Charlie said.

"How do you remember that, Dad?" I asked.

"I usually can't remember what I had for lunch, but I'll always remember what you did in that game," Dad said. "Coming up here to The Heart after games and bragging on you to Frank and some of the other guys was one of my favorite things to do." He and Charlie were both laughing, but I was speechless.

§

Mom was sick for about a year before she died. She was diagnosed with cancer and died eleven months later. Mom ran things at home and when she died, Dad didn't handle it well. He drank a lot, switching from beer to whiskey, and he rarely went into town. He lost weight, stopped shaving, and often wore the same clothes several days in a row.

One day, I got a call from Jess Kopinsky, one of Dad's friends in Mercer. Jess said that Dad looked real sick and he thought I should come up to talk to him about getting some help. When I got to the house late the next afternoon, Dad was unshaven and was passed out on the couch. It smelled like he had thrown up on himself.

After I got him sobered up, we talked about his weight loss, and the fact that he wasn't taking care of himself. Dad insisted that he was fine, just depressed without Mom. I told him that I thought it would be best for him to move down to Chicago so he could be nearer to me, but he wouldn't hear of it. When I left, I wasn't sure if I would see him alive again.

About three weeks later I got another call from Jess. It was a little after eleven o'clock at night and I had just gotten home from the office. Jess talked fast and I was having trouble making out what he was saying. What I did understand was that there had been a fire and Dad was in the hospital.

I threw a few things into a suitcase and headed north. The trip seemed to take forever, even though I was rushing to get to the hospital in Hurley. A couple of times I looked down at the speedometer and saw that I was going more than 90 miles per hour. I set the cruise control, and settled down for the long drive ahead.

When I finally got to the hospital, it was almost six o'clock in the morning and I was exhausted, but in a hurry. I rushed in through the automatic doors, and a cold, antiseptic smell hit me. I got directions to my dad's room and was standing in the doorway when a nurse asked if I needed help. I told her who I was and she told me that Dad was in a drug-induced coma. I sat down in the chair next to his bed and waited.

I couldn't be sure what time I fell asleep in the chair, but it was late in the afternoon when my dad's coughing woke me up. Two nurses rushed in to attend to him and his coughing eased. One of the nurses told me that

Dad's vitals were looking better, and that the doctor planned on bringing him out of the coma in the morning.

I slept in the chair next to Dad's bed that night and woke up before sunrise. A nurse stood next to me, taking Dad's pulse. My back was stiff, I was hungry, and I needed a shower. The nurse must have sensed my discomfort and asked if I'd like to use the visitor's shower down the hall. I told her that I absolutely would.

When I got back to Dad's room, the doctor was there and Dad was awake. He looked weak, his face pale and drawn.

"Hi, Kevin," Dad said in a raspy voice.

"Hi, Dad. How do you feel?

"Fantastic," he said. "How about you?"

We all laughed.

I sat with Dad for a couple of hours until he fell back to sleep. It was almost noon when I left the hospital to drive the twenty-some miles to Mercer to see what kind of damage the house had sustained.

Considering Dad's injuries, I knew the fire must have been bad, but I was surprised when I drove down the driveway to see nothing left of the house but the old brick chimney and a few charred two-by-fours sticking up here and there. Otherwise, the house was gone.

The smell of smoldering wood and the toxic ozone of burnt plastic filled the air as I walked around the ruins. I didn't dig through the rubble. It was obvious that everything in the house had been destroyed.

Back at the hospital, I told Dad what I had found. As could be expected, he was embarrassed. He said he had been cooking something on the stove and had fallen asleep on the couch. What he didn't say—what he didn't have to say—was that he was drunk when he had done this.

With nowhere else to go, Dad agreed to move into an independent living apartment near my home in Chicago. I knew he didn't want to, but I think the combination of the fire and the drugs they had him on helped to convince him that he really didn't have any other choice.

The move was good for Dad's health. He stopped drinking and started exercising, but it didn't do much for his spirits. He had been miserable ever since Mom's death, and living in Chicago, let alone in a tiny apartment, hadn't done anything to improve his disposition. Since he had moved to Chicago almost three years earlier, he hadn't been back to Mercer even once.

Dad didn't have much money, just a pension from the state and a monthly social security check. After he moved into the apartment, I mentioned that he should think about selling his property in Mercer. He had twenty-five acres of lakefront land and the value of the property had gone up substantially since he had purchased it.

"After I'm dead, you can do whatever you want with that property," he said. "But until then, I'm not selling it."

"Dad, you don't need that property right now, but you do need money to live on."

"Is that what this is about?" he asked. "You don't have to worry. I'll live in a tent back in Mercer if that's what it takes. You can stop paying for this hell hole anytime you want."

I tried to explain that I was only thinking about what was best for him, and that I didn't mind helping out with his living expenses, but Dad wasn't hearing any of it. That was the first and last time I ever brought up the idea of selling his property.

§

We checked into the Great Northern Lodge and got cleaned up to go out for German food at The Pines, one of our favorite restaurants in Mercer. The food was as good as I remembered. Dad got the beef rouladen, and I had the pork schnitzel. We saw several people we hadn't seen in years. Dad was in his element. He was back in Mercer, surrounded by friends. He laughed more talking to old friends while we were at dinner than I had seen him laugh in the previous three years.

When we were done eating, Dad said, "Kevin, what do you say we go have a drink at Club 51?"

Dad had already had a beer at The Heart and two more drinks with dinner. I knew he was having a good time, and I didn't feel like I was in a position to curb his fun. "Sure, let's go."

To our surprise, Club 51 was now called the Cranberry Inn. The whole place had been remodeled and was much lighter and more inviting than we had ever seen it. As soon as we walked in, Dad spotted Jess sitting with his wife, Maggie, at the bar. Jess was so excited he jumped up out of his chair and gave Dad a big bear hug.

"My God, Stan, it's so good to see you," Jess said. While Dad hugged Maggie, Jess gave me one of his bear hugs.

"What are you fellas doing back up in the Northwoods?" Maggie asked.

"I just couldn't stay away from you, Maggie," Dad said.

"It's good to see you're still full of shit," Maggie said, and we all laughed.

We joined Jess and Maggie at the bar, and they got us caught up on the latest gossip.

Some things about Mercer had changed since I left. For one, Billy Capone's old hotel with the Rathskeller Bar in the basement had been torn down, replaced by a gas station. I used to meet up with friends at The Rathskeller when I was home for breaks from college. Even the Great Northern Lodge, where we were staying, had been built since I moved to Chicago. There were a few other changes too, but overall the place had the same feel it had when I was a boy. Oddly, being back in town didn't feel bad at all.

§

The next day, we drove down County Road FF. The day was warm and the changing leaves were like an abstract water color, a blur of red, orange and yellow.

"God, I miss this place," Dad said.

"I forgot how beautiful it can be up here this time of year."

"Your mother and I used to spend our Sundays in the fall walking through the woods or driving the back roads. There's something about being out in nature that's good for the soul."

"Yeah," I said, "I guess there is."

As we turned onto the dirt road that led back to our old house, I could almost feel Dad's excitement. He rode with one hand on the door handle and tried to look everywhere at once.

The driveway was overgrown. We could still drive through, but weeds and grass were in the process of reclaiming the narrow dirt path. The parking area in front of the garage was almost completely covered with long, wispy grass.

When I parked the car, instead of eagerly jumping out like I expected, Dad sat quietly and scanned the scene. With the exception of the chimney, very little of the house still stood. The underbrush had crept out of the woods and was beginning to take over the area around the house and garage. The path leading down to the lake was hard to discern because of long grass and weeds.

Dad got out of the car and stood quietly looking around.

"Are you okay, Dad?" I asked.

He turned toward me, his eyes moist. "I guess it's not much to look at anymore, but it's still good to be here," he said.

We walked the perimeter of what used to be the house, stepping over burned boards and unidentifiable clods of charred debris. Dad leaned on the chimney and looked at me.

"The night the house burned down, I remember waking up, flames all around me. The smoke detector was going off and it made me think the phone was ringing. You know, I thought about just staying in the house. I was really missing your mom. But then I thought about you." Dad looked up at me and shrugged

"I'm glad you made it," I said. The moment called for a hug, but we'd never been the type of people who hugged.

"Let's go down to the dock," Dad said.

Although the path down to the lake was overgrown, it still felt familiar under my feet. I remembered the location of each rock and tree root. I was surprised that each twist and turn of the path was so fresh in my mind.

The dock wasn't in the lake. Someone had taken it out and stored it on the shore. If it had been left in the lake, the winter ice would have crushed it years earlier.

Just like the path, the edge of the lake had become overgrown. Dad ran his hand over the top of the long grass as he looked out at the water.

"There are a lot of memories out there in that water," he said. "You swam out there, you learned to ski, and I took you fishing for the first time. It feels like that lake is a part of our family."

When we first moved to Mercer, I spent my days down at the lake. I didn't know anyone, so the lake became my best friend. I went swimming or fishing or skiing. Whenever I was bored and needed a friend, the lake was there for me.

"We had a lot of good times out there," I said.

"I remember you, your mom and me sitting out on the dock one night," Dad said. "It was right after we moved up here. It was a clear night and there seemed to be more stars than I had ever seen. Then the Northern Lights started putting on a show for us. The sky turned pink and green, and the colors danced up above us. I was having doubts about our move to Mercer. I knew you were angry, missing Aurora, and I was worried about you. But when I saw those lights, I knew we had made the right decision."

"We didn't make the decision," I said. "You did."

"What do you mean?" Dad asked.

"You know what I mean," I said. "You made the decision to come up here after you cheated on Mom." The words were out of my mouth and I couldn't pull them back.

Dad seemed surprised. "Kevin, that's not how it was," he said. "Your mom and I made the best decision we could for the whole family."

I was suddenly a twelve-year-old boy in the body of a forty-six-year-old man. All of the old emotions, the anger, the bitterness, the frustration, came back to me in a flood. "Don't lie to me, Dad. I've known about you cheating on Mom for years. That was why we moved up here, not because you thought it would be good for us. You were running away from your affair."

"Kevin, that's not true. What you're saying, it didn't happen like that." Dad was hunched over, looking old and feeble.

"I don't want to talk about it anymore," I said. "Let's get going." I didn't want to make things worse. I turned and walked away from Dad.

"Kevin, wait..." Dad said, but I was already heading up the hill.

§

Back at the hotel, I told Dad that I had to call the office and it might take some time. I needed a break to calm down. I wasn't proud of my outburst, and I wanted to sort out my feelings.

Dad went up to our room, and I sat in the hotel lobby. My anger and resentment was still strong, and I didn't want to stay around Dad for fear that my emotions would boil over again.

When we first moved to Mercer, I was miserable. I missed my friends, I missed my home, and I missed the comfortable feeling I had knowing my way around the neighborhood. In Mercer, everything was new. I didn't know anyone and I didn't know the area. I was completely dependent on my parents for everything. Knowing why we had moved made things even worse, and resulted in me being constantly angry at my dad. In my eyes, nothing he ever did was right.

I couldn't tell Mom that I knew about Dad's affair. I didn't want to bring it up to her. Talking about it was like crossing some sort of line that a kid should never cross. Instead, I complained about Dad's decision to uproot us from our home.

Despite my constant complaining, I grew to like living in Mercer. I had a new group of friends and I had gained even more independence than I had in Aurora. Growing up on a lake surrounded by acres of woods just waiting to be explored was a great environment for a young boy. Even so, I could never forgive Dad, and I could never fully accept that Mercer was my home.

§

I sat in an overstuffed chair in the lobby, staring out at the lake behind the hotel. A young boy and his father were fishing from a canoe. Dad joined me, and we watched the father and son in silence for a few moments.

"Did you talk to your office?" he asked, breaking the silence.

I nodded, even though I hadn't bothered to make the call.

"I have a suggestion," Dad said. "I know we have reservations here at the hotel, but what do you think about staying at the house tonight?"

"There is no house," I said.

Dad laughed. "I didn't mean *in* the house. I was thinking we could camp out at the top of the hill in front of the garage. I'll bet we can rent a tent and sleeping bags at the sporting goods store."

"Do you feel up to sleeping on the ground?" I asked.

"Don't write me off yet," Dad said. "I'll be just fine.

I really wasn't in the mood to go camping, but I felt I owed Dad after my outburst. If sleeping in a tent at the house made him happy, then why not? "Well, if you think you'll be okay, then sure."

"Great," Dad said. "Let's go get what we need."

§

In town, we parked in front of the store that used to be called Mercer Sports. The sign indicated the new name was "Flowage Outfitters," and the building now had cedar siding and green shutters. It looked more rustic and inviting.

When we walked in we were greeted by an older woman. "Welcome to Flowage Outfitters," she said. "Can I help you find—Oh, aren't you Kevin Hargrove?"

"Yeah," I said, surprised to have been recognized. I looked closer at the woman and suddenly realized who it was.

"Wait here," she said. The woman rushed to the back of the store and in a moment, my old high school girlfriend, Annie, came out.

"Kevin!" Annie hugged me. "It's so good to see you. How are you?" Annie was talking fast, but her voice sounded exactly the same as it had in high school. She even smelled the same. I pulled back, realizing I'd been holding her embrace a bit too long.

"Hi Annie," I said. "I'm good. How are you?" I turned to the older woman. "Hi, Mrs. Hayes," I said, feeling like a teenage boy.

Mrs. Hayes hugged me and said, "I think you're old enough now that you can call me Emma."

Emma extended her hand to Dad. "Stan, it's nice to see you again." Annie gave him a hug.

"Do you own this place?" I asked.

"Mom and I moved back into town about a year ago and bought the store. We changed the name and cleaned it up a little. What brings you to town?"

"Just a visit. We came in to get some camping equipment."

"Well, you're in the right place," Emma said. "Stan, let me show you our camping section."

As Dad and Emma walked away, Annie grabbed my arm. "It's so good to see you," she said. "Tell me what's going on in your life."

"Well, I'm a lawyer in Chicago. I'm divorced and I work way too much. That's my life in a nutshell. How about you?"

Annie had been divorced for almost fifteen years. She and her mom had moved in together in Colorado, but after a while had decided to move back to Mercer. "We came back for a visit, and ended up buying the store and moving back," she said.

"Do you liking living in Mercer again?"

"I forgot how much I loved living here," Annie said. "And working with Mom has been a lot of fun. It's been a good move for both of us. Do you like living in Chicago?"

"I never gave it much thought. I mostly just go to work and then go back home."

"I was always surprised you moved away."

"I couldn't wait to get away from here," I said.

"I thought you loved living here."

"Yeah, that's what my dad thought too. Have you two been talking?" We both laughed.

"We're all set," Dad said, as he and Emma walked to the front of the store where Annie and I still stood. "We just need to drive around back to load up the car."

"Stan had a great idea," Emma said. "After the two of you go set up camp, we're all going to get together for supper at the Ding-A-Ling."

"That sounds great," Annie said.

"We'll meet you at the restaurant at about seven. Will that work?" Dad asked.

"It will," Annie said, her smile reminding me of the girl I had once spent so much time with.

Dad nodded. "Kevin, let's get the gear loaded up. We still need to stop at Snow's to get food and then we can go make camp."

§

Annie Hayes moved to Mercer from Colorado when we were both sophomores in high school. We became friends because we both liked sports and both played on the school's basketball teams. We started dating that year and continued dating straight through to graduation.

Annie had a terrific sense of humor, often playing practical jokes on me and her other friends. She was a natural athlete who didn't have any pretenses. She was a beautiful girl, with long ginger blond hair and a slim, fit body, but she never felt like she had to be all made up or wear fancy clothes. Everything about her was natural and understated.

After high school, I moved to Madison to attend the University of Wisconsin, and Annie went to the University of Colorado. We agreed that we'd keep dating, but it was difficult to sustain a relationship being that far apart.

The letters were frequent at first. We wrote to each other once or twice a week. In time, that dwindled down to a letter every couple of weeks and then maybe one per month. Right after we started college, Annie's dad died, and her mom and younger brother moved back to Colorado. So even during school breaks, we didn't get the chance to see each other.

I was lonely in Madison without Annie. I could have dated other women, but I didn't want to go out with anyone else. When we were in high school, Annie and I talked about someday getting married, and although our talk of marriage faded once we were in college, I couldn't help but feel like we were still going to end up together.

After freshman year, we talked about seeing each other during the summer, but it never happened. At the start of my second year in college, the tone of Annie's letters changed. She wrote like a friend rather than a girlfriend, and, although I looked forward to her letters, it broke my heart to read them.

When I didn't get a letter from Annie for several weeks, and couldn't contact her by phone, I borrowed a friend's car and drove to Boulder. I had made up my mind that if she was still interested, I was going to transfer to the University of Colorado to be near her.

Annie was surprised to see me. She answered the door wearing a gray University of Colorado sweatshirt and a pair of black sweatpants. Her hair was pulled back in a ponytail. She was even more beautiful than I remembered.

"My God! Kevin, what are you doing here?" I had expected a kiss or at least a hug, but Annie just stood at the doorway, staring.

"I came to see you," I said, and leaned forward to kiss her. Annie turned her head, gave me a quick hug, and then backed away. She invited me in, and right away I knew something wasn't right.

"Kevin, I'd like you to meet Aaron. Aaron, this is Kevin. He's an old high school friend from Wisconsin."

A tall, good looking guy stood up from the couch and shook my hand. "Nice to meet you, Kevin."

"Nice to meet you," I said, mumbling.

Aaron looked the way I thought a guy from Colorado should look, with a big mop of dark hair and a physique built by hiking mountain trails and gliding down ski slopes. I immediately hated him.

"It's good to see you, Kevin," Annie said, moving next to Aaron, "and I have some news for you." She grabbed Aaron's hand and sat next to him on the couch. "Aaron and I are engaged. We're going to be married next summer."

Annie kept talking, but what she said didn't register. I remember shaking Aaron's hand again and saying something about being happy for them. I wanted to be anywhere but there. I don't remember leaving.

§

Annie was engaged and the hope that I had for a future with her was now dead. Rather than heading back to school, I drove to Mercer. I wasn't sure why. I didn't think it through. I just wanted to be where I felt comfortable and safe.

I pulled into town at about seven o'clock in the morning. Rather than going home, I drove down to Lake of the Falls Park. It was one of my favorite places in Mercer, and it was a place where I could be by myself to think.

The morning was cool and a thin fog hung over the water of the falls. I put on a sweatshirt and sat down on a large rock near the water. There was patchy snow along the bank, and the rich, loamy smell of the ground hugged the air. New leaves were beginning to appear on the otherwise bare branches of sugar maple trees, and a few brave buds were beginning to blossom on the opposite side of the falls.

What now? I didn't know what to do. My future had been tied up in Annie. Without her, I didn't want to do anything, including going back to school. Of course, I didn't have many options. I could either return to school or move back home.

If Annie wasn't going to be a part of my future, then what did the future hold? The thoughts and questions came too quickly. My brain was too garbled to make sense of it all.

I sat watching the water roll over the rocks, the fresh morning air clearing my head. I felt a quiet come over me. I can't say I felt happy, but I had a feeling envelop me that said without words, *You're going to be all right.*

I had my doubts. My heart had just been broken, and I was confused about the future. Even so, being back in Mercer near the rushing water calmed me, and gave me a sense of peace. I desperately wanted to believe what the falls were telling me.

§

At dinner, Dad and Emma carried on a conversation about Dad's days as a forest ranger, and Annie and I talked like we had never been apart, reminiscing about our high school days, and sharing regrets over our failed marriages.

"I was too young when we got married," Annie said. "I didn't think so at the time, but I know it now."

I nodded. There was a lot I could tell Annie about how I had single-handedly ruined my marriage, or about how my father's infidelity had left me doubting whether marriage was even a worthwhile endeavor, but I didn't want her to see that side of me. It felt good to have someone see me the way I used to be.

As we talked, Lori Briggs, a classmate of ours from high school, spotted us. She was tall and thin, with dark hair and an overbite.

"Oh my gosh, Annie and Kevin! It's so good to see you," Lori said.

Annie remembered Lori, and I think she sensed that I didn't, so she introduced her to Emma and Dad as a way of letting me know Lori's name.

"I don't want to keep you from your meal. I just wanted to say hi and tell you how good it is to see you back together."

My mouth opened, but no words came out. Annie put her hand on my arm and said, "It was good seeing you, Lori."

When Lori walked away, Annie patted my arm and said, "You're not going to hyperventilate, are you? You look kind of pale." She laughed.

"Annie, she thought we were together," I said.

"That's okay. It will give her something to talk about with her friends." Annie smiled, just as confident as I remembered.

After dinner, I had another beer, and Annie had a glass of wine. It was amazing how she talked to me as if there hadn't been a twenty-five year gap in our relationship. I was so engrossed in my conversation with her that I almost forgot that Emma and Dad were still at the table with us.

"I'm going to give Stan a ride home," Emma said. "You two can stay and talk, but us old folks need our rest. Kevin, do you mind giving Annie a ride home?"

"No," I said, somewhat caught off guard. "No, that's—Annie, do you want to stick around for a while?" I felt like a shy teenager again.

"Sure," Annie said. "You guys go ahead. Kevin can drop me off later."

After Emma and Dad left, Annie and I gave up our table and took seats at one end of the restaurant's half-circle bar.

"What was the deal with you when we were talking to Lori?" Annie asked.

"What do you mean?"

"You were so shocked when she thought we were a couple."

"It didn't dawn on me that anyone would think we were together like that.

"It was funny watching you squirm." We both laughed.

"Why didn't you tell her the truth?" I asked.

"Lori's a big gossip. I figured I'd give her something to gossip about. You weren't embarrassed, were you?"

"No, just surprised." I finished my beer, and asked Annie if she wanted another glass of wine.

"Let's go for a drive," Annie said.

"Where do you want to go?"

"Let's just drive around a little. It will be easier to talk away from so many people."

As we drove, Annie pointed out different landmarks and we recalled stories from our high school days, faded memories of snowball fights in the high school parking lot, shooting baskets at Carow Park, and making out in the woods near Rice Lake.

"See that empty building right there?" Annie asked. We were driving through town on Route 51and Annie was pointing at a green, wood-sided building.

"Yeah, that used to be Carl Lawson's law office, wasn't it?"

"It was up until about a year ago," Annie said. "Carl and his wife moved to Arizona. His wife wasn't in the best of health, and Carl was seventy-five. He figured it was time to retire."

"Really? What do people do for a lawyer now?"

"They either go up to Hurley or down to Minocqua. Carl was the only lawyer in town."

"Hmm," I said, not knowing what else to say.

"You know, you could move up here and start your own law practice," Annie said.

"I have my Wisconsin license, but I don't think there's much call up here for the kind of law I practice."

"Well, it's just an idea." Annie said.

We drove to the house on Echo Lake Annie shared with her mom.

"Would you like to sit on the dock for a while?" she asked.

I said I would, and we walked around the house to the back yard. The moon sparkled on the water and moonlight seemed to come from across the lake right up to Annie's house. Her canoe lay upside down on the shore, and a small bass boat was tied to the dock. The boat bobbed quietly in the water. I sat on a wooden bench that was anchored to one side of the dock, and Annie sat next to me.

"Sitting like this, looking at the stars and the water, I think that's what I missed most when I moved to Colorado."

It's nice," I said. "I can see why you missed it."

"I know we were young," Annie said, "but I never apologized to you when I went off to Colorado and got engaged. The truth is, I didn't have the guts to tell you. I was shocked when you showed up at my apartment door. I had made myself believe that you knew we weren't together any more. I really am sorry about that, Kevin."

Annie's apology was unnecessary, but it reminded me how bad it hurt when she gave me the news that she was getting married. "You don't have to apologize. That was a long time ago. I'm almost over it." I laughed.

Annie bumped my shoulder with hers, and scooted closer to me on the bench. "Well, I am sorry. More than you know."

"What do you mean?"

Nearby, a loon gave out a call that sounded like a crazy laugh, and then the night went quiet again. Annie leaned against me, and threaded her arm through mine.

"My marriage wasn't a very happy one," she said. "After we married, Aaron changed. His dark side came out. He was a pretty heavy drinker, and he used to get drunk and berate me. He'd tell me I wasn't as pretty as one woman he used to go out with, or as good in bed as another. He never hit me, but I was often scared that he would."

"That's horrible, Annie. I'm sorry you had to go through that."

"Then I found out he was having an affair. I confronted him, and he apologized. Said he'd never do that again. I was a fool and believed him. A few years later, he cheated again, and that was the end of our marriage."

I felt awful for Annie. Whatever problems Rebecca and I had, at least there was no verbal abuse, and nobody cheated. I shifted on the bench, and squeezed Annie's arm with mine.

"You know the worst part?" she asked. "I didn't leave him. He left me. I was ready to forgive him again, but he wanted to marry the bimbo he was seeing."

"Why do you think you didn't want to divorce him after what he did?" I immediately regretted the question. It was none of my business, and I didn't want to make Annie talk about things she'd prefer to keep locked away. Like always, Annie was an open book.

"I'll never understand what I was thinking. I wanted to do whatever was necessary to keep us together. I was in love, and I was totally committed to our marriage." Annie took a deep breath, and looked up at the starry sky. She seemed to be gathering her thoughts, so I kept quiet.

"In hindsight, I should have ended the marriage long before it fell apart, but I didn't," she said. "Even after the way Aaron treated me, it took me a long time to get over our divorce. I should have been happy to be away from him, but instead, I felt like a failure."

I wondered if Rebecca felt that way: sad to be divorced, but happy to be away from me.

"I'm not sure why I grieved so much," Annie said. "It was a long time ago, and I guess the grieving was necessary. I'm just glad that part of my life is in the distant past. Things are much, much better now."

Annie had sounded sad and injured while she told me about her marriage, but now she was back to her positive, confident self. She leaned over and kissed me softly on the lips. The kiss was unexpected, and I leaned away from her. She opened her eyes, and, looking into them, I could see the woman I had once loved. Part of me wanted to kiss her, to hold her again in my arms. The other part wanted to warn her about me, to tell her that

I wasn't good at relationships, and that she should run away as fast as she could. I made my decision. Holding her face in my hands, I kissed her, and felt the feelings from so long ago stirring again.

Annie smiled, and repositioned herself so she was leaning against me, her arm once again intertwined with mine. I could feel the warmth of her body. "Am I going to see you again tomorrow?" she asked.

"I don't know what Dad has planned, but why don't we have dinner tomorrow night?"

"Dinner? You really have turned into a Chicagoan," she said with a laugh. "We still call it supper up here."

"Okay. Let's have supper tomorrow night."

"Sounds good," she said, leaning her head on my shoulder.

The loon called out again. From somewhere off in the distance, another loon answered with a mournful wail, like a wolf's howl, and then the lake went quiet again.

§

When I woke the next morning, Dad was already up making breakfast over an open fire. He looked more alive than I had seen him in a long time.

"Good morning, Kevin. How did you sleep?"

"Pretty good," I said, rubbing my eyes. "You?"

"That was the best sleep I've had in a long time. I feel ten years younger this morning."

The smell of wood smoke and bacon filled the early morning air. Dad poured a cup of coffee into one of the Styrofoam cups we had purchased at the grocery store, and handed it to me. "This should help you wake up."

Dad served the eggs and bacon, and sat down in a lawn chair. "How did it go with you and Annie?"

"It was good to see her again. It was certainly unexpected," I said with a bit of a laugh.

"I'll bet. She hasn't changed much since high school. She still has those bright eyes and that fun-loving personality."

"Yeah, it almost felt like we were back in high school. It was kind of weird."

"What do you mean?" Dad asked, eating his eggs.

"I don't know. Just being back up here, seeing Annie. Everything just felt weird."

Dad let out a little laugh. "So what's on the agenda for today?"

"Annie wants to go have dinner—I mean, supper—tonight. Does that sound okay with you?" I asked.

"Actually, I'd like to just spend some time here, maybe clean the place up a little bit. Plus, you don't need an old man tagging along on your date. You two go and have a good time."

"It's not really a date—"

"It should be," he said.

I laughed. "Yeah, maybe it should."

"I'd like you to do me a favor this afternoon. If you don't mind, could you drive me over to the bank and then out to Lake of the Falls Park?"

"Sure," I said, taking a sip of my coffee.

"Great," he said, then turned to stare out at the lake, the early morning sun glinting off the water.

§

Dad went into the bank while I stayed in the car. Despite the fact that he had lived in Chicago for three years, he still did his banking in Mercer.

From the parking lot, I watched cars go by. Traffic was light. The day was warm and sunny, but there were very few people on the street. Most of the summer tourists were gone, their cabins closed up waiting for the winter snow to come. It was in-between seasons when things really slowed down in town.

Dad came out of the bank, and we drove in silence to the park. I knew my words from the previous day had hurt him, and I regretted it. I needed to apologize.

At the park, Dad asked me to pull over just past the bridge that crossed the falls. He got out of the car, walked down the bank to sit on a large boulder, and stared into the water.

The park had changed some since I had been there last. The covered wooden bridge had been replaced by a concrete bridge built for snowmobilers. The parking area wasn't as rustic as it had once been. But what hadn't changed was the peace I felt when I got near the falls. There was a positive energy, a kind of life force, at the falls that I never felt anywhere else.

Dad said he needed a minute by himself, so when I got out of the car, rather than going to be near him, I stood on the concrete bridge, and stared down into the falls.

The water tumbled over the rocks directly below me and the sound of the falls was all I could hear. To the north was the calm water of the Turtle River, and beyond that, Lake of the Falls. Below the falls, the Turtle River ambled south toward the Turtle-Flambeau Flowage.

I looked down where Dad was still sitting on the rock. The sound of the water engulfed me and I closed my eyes. I felt the peace of the falls surround me, washing away the last remnants of those earlier emotions. Dad had made a mistake nearly forty years earlier, but a lot of time had passed, and he'd become an old man. It was time to let go of the resentment I'd felt toward him for so many years.

I don't know how long I stood on the bridge with my eyes closed. When I opened them, Dad was still sitting on the rock at the base of the falls. I walked down to join him.

Before I could say anything, Dad said, "I used to come out here a lot when you were young. Every time I had a problem, whether something had happened at work or your mom and I had a fight or it was something with you, I would come out here to sit on this rock and stare at the falls. I'm not sure how it started, but it seemed like every time I came out here, I felt better. I didn't always come away with the answers I was looking for, but I knew that things would work out."

I started to speak, but Dad put up his hand.

"You surprised me yesterday at the house when you got angry," he said. "I was surprised that you thought we moved up here because I cheated on your mom. That's not true, Kevin. I never cheated on your mom.

"But I heard you and Mom talking about it."

"I had hoped I'd never have to share this with you," Dad said, holding up an envelope, "but I guess it's time you knew the truth."

He handed me the envelope, and I could see it had my name on it. The handwriting was Mom's.

"What is this?"

"Open it and find out."

I opened the envelope and inside was a handwritten letter in blue ink on lined, white paper. I unfolded it, and began to read.

Dear Kevin,

I asked your father to give this to you after I was gone. This is the most difficult letter I have ever written, but you need to know the truth.

For years, you have hated your father for moving us to Mercer. I thought that you would eventually get used to your new home, but even after living here for several years, you still held a grudge against your dad. I allowed you to complain to me about him all of those years, but I never had the courage to tell you the truth. It's time to set the record straight.

I know that you're still angry at your father for moving us to Mercer, but the truth is, we moved to Mercer because of me, not your father. As embarrassed as I am to admit it, I had an affair when you were very young, and it almost destroyed our family. Your father and I wanted a fresh start. He was forgiving enough to give me a second chance. So when he got a job with the state, we decided to start over in Mercer.

You see, I was the cause of our move. I have spent my life trying to make up for my selfish mistake, and have done my best to be a loving wife and mother. I pray that my confession, as late as it is, will help you to know the truth, and forgive your father.

With all the love in my heart,

Mom

I was disoriented. Everything I had thought I knew about my family growing up was wrong. My dad wasn't the bad guy I had believed him to be, and even if I tried, I could never think badly about my mom. I spent all of those years wanting to punish my dad, but instead, just made myself miserable.

I looked up from the letter, my eyes moist, unable to speak.

"Don't judge your mom too harshly," Dad said. "She was a wonderful woman, and, at the time, she had a horrible husband. But we loved each other and we found a way to hold our family together."

"I don't know what to say, Dad," I said, shaking my head. "I'm so sorry."

Dad waved his hand, dismissing my apology. "You don't need to apologize. That was a long time ago." He put his arm around my shoulder, and smiled. "We'd better head back, he said. "You've got to get ready for your date."

§

I pulled into Annie's driveway, and, before I could get out of the car, the front door opened, and Annie came bounding down the stairs. She wore faded jeans and a blue top with a white sweater around her shoulders. Her ginger blond hair was down and curled. She slid into the passenger seat and turned toward me with a big smile. "Hi, Kevin."

"Hi," I said. "Where's your mom?"

"I'm a big girl. She lets me go out on my own now," Annie said. We both laughed.

"I thought she was going to go with us."

"No. Mom said she didn't want to get in the way. Where's your dad?"

"He's back at the house. Or at least where the house used to be. When I left, he was cooking a steak over an open fire and was happy as a clam."

"It looks like it's just you and me and no chaperones tonight." Annie suggested we drive out to Lake of the Falls Park so we could talk.

When we got there, I parked in the same place I had parked earlier that afternoon with Dad. Annie got out of the car and I followed her down to the water.

Annie turned toward me and sat down on the same rock Dad had sat on earlier. Her back was to the water. "I don't know what it is about this place, but it always helps me to relax and think clearly," she said.

"I used to come out here when I was a kid," I said. "Whenever I had a problem or there was something I had on my mind, I'd get on my bike and ride down here. This is the rock I used to sit on."

"Really? I guess it's a special place for both of us," Annie said. "I'm surprised we never ran into each other here." We both laughed.

"Kevin, I've been thinking all day and I want to say something to you. I'm afraid you're going to think I'm nuts or something, but I'm just going to come out and say it."

"I'm not going to think you're nuts. What's on your mind?"

"I've thought a lot about what I said last night, you know, about you buying Carl Lawson's old office and starting your own law practice up here. The more I think about it, the better I like the idea."

"You *are* nuts," I said, laughing. Annie punched me on the arm.

"Seriously, just think about it. You could move up here with your dad. You know he's just dying to get back. The area needs a lawyer. It could work out great."

"And I could see you," I said.

"Yeah," Annie said softly. "I know we were just kids, but I made a big mistake when I let you go before. I don't want to make that same mistake again."

Annie didn't know me anymore, and I didn't want her to be surprised or disappointed. "I'm not the same person you used to know, Annie. I work way too much. I'm uptight. I don't socialize at all. I'm really not much fun."

Annie laughed. "That's in Chicago. Up here, you're already turning back into the person you used to be."

I wanted to argue with her, but she had a point. During my time in Mercer, I hadn't thought about work at all. Normally, if I was out of the office, I'd call back every few hours. But since I had been back, I hadn't called at all.

"You think letting me go was a mistake?" I asked.

"Maybe the biggest mistake of my life. I've had a lot of years to think about it, Kevin, and I know that I don't want to let you go again."

It was starting to get dark. The sunset in the distance was a brilliant mixture of orange and blue. Dad loved these kinds of sunsets. He always said they were an omen of better times ahead.

"Well, you certainly have given us something to talk about," I said. "What do you say we go get dinner and talk about it some more?"

"Supper, Kevin. Supper."

"Oh, right. Let's get supper and talk about it some more."

"That sounds good. I'll race you to the car," she said, getting a head start on me.

"You still cheat," I said, and we both ran toward the car, laughing.

§

We got back to Chicago late on Sunday afternoon. I dropped Dad off at his apartment with a promise that I wouldn't be such a stranger. He wasn't happy about being back in the city, but the trip had rejuvenated him. He stood up straighter, walked with a purpose, and smiled at the people in his apartment building as he passed them in the hall. I was pleased with and surprised by his new attitude.

I called Annie that night and she told me she missed me. I missed her too. Before Dad and I left Mercer, we stopped by her house to say our goodbyes. Annie gave me a big going away kiss, and made me promise to come back soon. I hated the feeling of leaving her.

The next few days at work were crazy. Because I had been gone, meetings got backed up and we had to squeeze them in without disrupting our normal schedule. I was forced to work late into the night to catch up, and my calls to Annie became shorter and shorter. I told Dad I would have dinner with him on the Friday after we returned from our trip, but then had to cancel our plans so I could catch up on paperwork. I thought I might be able to see him during the weekend, but I wound up working both Saturday and Sunday.

I was at the office the next Monday when Annie called. I was in the middle of a meeting, and asked my secretary to tell her I would return her call that night. When I finally got around to calling her, she was already in bed.

"I'm really sorry, Annie. I meant to call earlier."

"You warned me that all you do is work," she said.

I wanted to respond, but couldn't think of anything intelligent to say.

"Am I going to see you soon?" she asked.

I had been trying to figure out when I could get back up to Mercer, but hadn't yet found a good time. "I know I can't this weekend. One of our clients has a big filing coming up at the end of the month and we have to get everything done."

"You don't think you can get up here before the end of the month?" Annie asked.

"No, I don't think so." There was an uncomfortable silence. I wanted to see Annie badly, but I knew I couldn't get away for at least a couple of weeks. "Is there any chance you can come to Chicago?"

"Maybe," she said. "Things are slow at the store right now. Mom can probably handle a weekend without me."

We made plans for Annie to visit two weekends later. I looked forward to her visit, but couldn't shake the nagging feeling that I wasn't ready for another relationship. My track record wasn't good, and I wasn't convinced that I had changed since my days with Rebecca. I wasn't sure that I could.

§

Annie drove to Rhinelander—the closest commercial airport to Mercer—and flew into Chicago. I picked her up at Midway, and helped her put her suitcase in the trunk of my car. I swung out into traffic on Cicero Avenue, and then on to the Stevenson Expressway. Annie sat as close to me as the bucket seats would allow, and we held hands as I drove.

Traffic was slow and heavy, normal for a Friday afternoon. Annie talked about the store, and her mom, and the latest gossip from Mercer. I was only too happy to listen.

I had told Annie before she made plans to visit that I would have to get some work done on Friday afternoon, but that I'd devote the rest of the weekend to her. I was glad she was so understanding. I had several files to work on, and I was anxious to get back to my house to dig into them.

As I worked, Annie sat on the couch in the living room and read a book she brought with her. When she tired of that, she came into my office and put her arms around my shoulders, kissing my neck.

"Do you mind if I listen to some music?" she asked.

"Go ahead. You know how to work the stereo?"

"I'll figure it out. You just get your work done so you can wine and dine me."

When she got bored listening to Don Henley and Fleetwood Mac, she poked her head into the office and said, "I'm going to go for a walk."

"Okay, I'll see you in a little bit," I said, without looking up.

I was on the phone with Phil Bloom, one of the attorneys from my office, when I heard the front door open. "Are you still working?" Annie called from the living room. I didn't answer, so she came into the office and found me on the phone. "Sorry," she mouthed, and put her hands up in apology.

When I got off the phone, I went into the living room, and found Annie asleep on the couch. The sun had gone down and the room was dark. I thought about waking her, but instead I let her sleep and went back into the office to do some more work.

I was excited to have Annie in my house, but it was also a little disconcerting. I looked forward to having Annie with me and being able to share my life with her. I loved the thought of it. But I had been alone for a long time, and having her in the house put a pressure on me that I hadn't felt in quite a while. I had to think about someone other than myself, and it was a strange and chaffing feeling.

When Annie woke, she walked down the hall into my office. "What time is it?" she asked, yawning.

"I didn't want to wake you," I said, looking at my watch. "It's twenty after nine."

"Is it too late to eat? I'm starved."

I laughed. "This isn't Mercer. They don't roll up the streets when the sun goes down. You can eat whenever you're hungry."

"We don't roll up the streets," she said. "Are you going to feed me?"

We went to Chicago Pizza and Oven Grinder around the corner from my house. We each ordered a half-pound pizza pot pie and shared a chef's salad. While we waited, I had a beer and Annie had a glass of wine.

"Do you eat here very often?" she asked.

"I haven't been here in a while. I'm usually still at the office around dinner time. If I eat at all, I usually eat over there."

"Why do you work so much?

"It's just what the job requires," I said. Rebecca used to ask the same question. The thought made me uncomfortable and I wanted to change the subject. "How was your walk?"

"It was good. Your neighborhood is really nice. Nicer and cleaner than I expected."

"Cleaner?"

"When I think about the city, I think about everything being dirty. I've always had a bias against big cities."

"I thought that way before I moved here. But really, it's not that bad."

"I suppose not, but I don't think I could ever get used to it."

I had this idea in the back of my head that maybe, given enough time, I could talk Annie into moving to Chicago. I wanted a future with her, and, long term, we couldn't have much of a relationship being six hours apart. Her comment threw cold water on my hopes to get her to move near me.

After dinner, we went for a walk down North Clark Street. Despite the late hour, there were still a lot of people on the street, and the bars and restaurants did a brisk business.

"Isn't this nice, having so many places to go this late at night?" I asked.

"It's nice to visit, but even if I lived here, I can't imagine taking advantage of it very often. Do you go out much?"

"No, but it's nice having all of this here if you want it."

"Don't get me wrong, I like going out like this once in a while, but most of the time, I'd rather just go out behind the house and sit on the dock. I like to watch the stars."

I looked up at the sky, but couldn't see any stars because of the city lights. Annie saw me look up, but didn't say anything. She held my hand a little tighter and snuggled up closer to me.

We got back home around midnight. I poured each of us a glass of wine and we sat on the couch, our feet up on the coffee table. As we talked, I felt myself starting to fall asleep. It had been a long day and I was tired. Annie sat up and put her wine glass on the table. She took mine and set it next to hers. She swung a leg over me and sat on my thighs facing me. "Don't fall asleep on me yet," she said, unbuttoning my shirt. "I have plans for you."

§

When I woke the next morning, I was lying on my back and Annie was lying next to me on her stomach, her arm stretching across the bed and her hand resting on my chest. The previous night had been a pleasant surprise. When Annie agreed to visit, I wasn't even sure we would sleep in the same room. I had made up the bed in the guest room just in case.

Of course, this wasn't the first time we'd had sex, but it had been many years, and back then we were young and unsure of ourselves. As adults, we knew what we wanted, and the previous night's activities had been a much more satisfying experience.

Annie was a more insistent lover than Rebecca had been. One wasn't better than the other. They were just different. Rebecca was more willing to follow my lead, to come along for the ride. Annie was more apt to take the lead and control our interplay. Their bodies were different, too. Rebecca was soft curves, and slow, fluid movements. Annie was angular, with more aggressive, purposeful movements.

I snuck out from under Annie's hand without waking her and went down to my office. She wanted to visit the zoo, and I wanted to get some work done before we went. I had been working for about an hour when Annie wandered into the room.

"Good morning." Annie wore one of my light blue dress shirts and her hair was wild. The shirt hung down almost to her knees. When I turned, she sat down on my lap and gave me a kiss. "Why didn't you wake me?"

"I thought you could use some sleep," I said.

"We need to get going. I don't want to miss the zoo."

"It's not going anywhere. Why don't you get ready and I'll finish up here."

Annie gave me another kiss and then went upstairs to take a shower. Through the ceiling, I could hear her singing "Girls Just Want to Have Fun," and I imagined her naked under the spray of the showerhead. I thought about joining her, but I wanted to finish the brief I was working on before we left for the zoo.

I was on the phone with Phil when Annie came into the office ready to go. She wore faded jeans, a pink sweatshirt, and a Cubs cap. Her hair was pulled back in a ponytail and stuck out through the hole in the back of the cap. I held up my index finger to indicate I would be just a minute. Annie sat down in a recliner I kept in the office, but when I didn't get off the phone after several minutes, she got up and left the room. When I finally got off the phone, I found Annie sitting on the couch in the living room looking at a framed photo.

"Is this Rebecca?" she asked, handing me the photo.

"That was taken a couple of years before we split up. Where'd you find it?"

"I was looking for the TV remote and found it in the drawer under the TV. Sorry, I shouldn't have been snooping."

"No, that's okay. I haven't seen this in years."

"Why did you guys split up?"

I put the photo back in the drawer and sat next to Annie on the couch. "It was my fault," I said. "I didn't put enough effort into the marriage and it eventually ended." Annie didn't need to know all of the details about what a poor husband I had been.

§

Our day at the zoo was pleasant enough, but Annie wasn't being her usual fun-loving self. She was quiet and seemed to be lost in thought much of the time. I wasn't the best company either. Twice I took calls from my office, and talked both times for several minutes while Annie milled about by herself, watching the monkeys or lions laze in the mid-day sun.

We went to Café Ba-Ba-Reeba's for dinner. I hadn't been there before, but I heard it was a fun, casual place that served Spanish tapas. The place was packed, and we were lucky to get a table. Annie started with chicken and ham croquetas, and I had goat cheese baked in tomato sauce. We ordered a pitcher of classic red sangria.

I wanted to cheer Annie up, but I wasn't sure what to do. When I asked what was wrong, she insisted everything was okay. I knew better, but what could I say?

Next, Annie ordered paella valenciana with roasted pork, txistorra sausage, and braised pork belly. It was a meat lover's dream come true. I got skewered chicken and chorizo sausage.

As we ate, Annie came out of her shell a little bit, most likely from the sangria, which she seemed to enjoy. The fun, energetic vibe of the restaurant helped to pick up her spirits too. When we had finished our tapas, Annie moved closer to me and put her head on my shoulder.

"I've had fun being with you this weekend. I wish you could come back with me tomorrow."

"I wish you could stay with me instead of going back north."

"I think we've had this conversation before," she said.

I tried to think of a reply that wouldn't ruin the mood when the server came by to take our dessert order. Annie ordered the chocolate truffle cake, and I got the apple empanada with vanilla ice cream.

"You were about to say?" Annie asked.

Before I could respond, my phone rang. I could see from the caller ID that it was Phil, and I knew he wouldn't be calling so late on a Saturday night if it wasn't very important.

"I'm sorry, Annie. I have to take this." I got up from the table and went outside to answer the call.

I wasn't gone more than ten or fifteen minutes, but I returned to a changed Annie. "Sorry about that," I said, sitting down.

"Oh, I understand," she said, a noticeable slur to her words. Annie had a half-full tumbler of sangria in her hand, and the heavy glass pitcher sat empty on the table. "This is what your life is like now, isn't it? If you're not sleeping, you're working."

I hesitated to answer. I didn't want to lie, but I didn't want to upset her more. "Yeah, I guess it is."

"That's too bad, Kevin. You used to be a lot of fun."

§

We were supposed to go to brunch on Sunday morning, but Annie begged off, saying she was still full from dinner the previous night. I worked in the office while she got ready for her flight back to Wisconsin. We barely spoke.

When we got in the car to head to the airport, Annie took my hand, and looked up at me as I maneuvered my way through Chicago traffic. "I'm sorry for what I said last night, Kevin. I was out of line."

"You don't need to apologize. What you said was true. Probably eighty or ninety percent of my time is spent either sleeping or working."

Annie shook her head. "It might be true, but it wasn't my place to point it out, especially in such a nasty way."

I brought Annie's hand to my mouth and kissed it. "I'd love to tell you that things are going to change, but I don't know if that's going to happen. There always seems to be more work to do."

She nodded, and we rode to the airport in silence.

§

A week after Annie's visit, I was traveling with Phil to meet with a client, and we had a three hour drive each way. We talked about our personal lives as we drove.

"I think my kids hate me. They don't ever have anything to say, except if they need money. I've become more of a bank to them than a father."

Phil had two grown kids from a previous marriage and three teenagers with his current wife. "I'm sure they don't hate you," I said.

"Don't be so sure. They tolerate me because I put a roof over their heads, food on the table, and cell phones in their ears. Even if they don't hate me, I know they resent me."

"Why would they resent you?"

Phil looked at me and smiled. "You're kidding, right?"

I shook my head. "No. What do you mean?"

"They resent me because I'm never home. I can't ever make it to their concerts or ball games. We make plans and I end up canceling or they go without me. You know what it was like with you and Rebecca? Now add in a few kids and think of how bad it would be."

I thought back to my time with Rebecca. I was thankful we didn't have kids when we split. "What are you going to do about it?" I asked.

"Nothing. I'm stuck on the hamster wheel and it just keeps going around and around. I can't jump off. Connie and the kids are too used to their lifestyle. You think they're going to give up their comfortable lives so I can 'find myself?'" Phil raised his hands and made the "air quote" sign. "Not a chance. The sad truth is, we make our choices and then we have to live with the consequences."

I shook my head. "There must be a better way."

"There is. Don't get on the wheel in the first place, and if you have the opportunity to get off, don't miss your chance."

I didn't know if Phil was talking about my specific situation or just making general conversation, but his words hit home. I had the opportunity to get off the wheel. My house was paid off, I didn't owe anything on my car, and I had enough money in retirement. Why did I keep working these ridiculous hours to make money that, although I liked, I really didn't need? I was building a bank account, not a life.

There was no doubt that I could use a change. I had been in a rut so long that I didn't even think about getting out any more. Annie made me think about getting out.

§

Dad and I made plans to have dinner a few nights after my talk with Phil. I had deadlines to meet, and really needed to work late, but I left the office anyway to meet up with Dad. When I saw him, I could tell he had lost some of the glow he had when we first returned from Mercer.

"I'm glad you were able to get away tonight," Dad said. "Things slowed down at work?"

"Not really, but I've been neglecting you, and I wanted to talk to you about something."

"I'm all ears."

"Did you know that Carl Lawson's old office up in Mercer is empty?" I asked.

"Yeah, I heard he moved to Arizona. I don't think Lillie was doing very well."

"Annie has this crazy idea about me opening a law practice up there. She thinks I should buy Carl's old office. What do you think?"

"I don't think it's crazy," he said. "Are you thinking about it?"

"Yeah, I am."

"I know it would be a lot of driving going between here and Mercer," he said. "Are you thinking about just being in the office up there a few days each month?"

"No, what I'm actually thinking about is quitting the law firm here and moving up to Mercer full time."

Dad looked confused. "Move to Mercer full time?" he asked.

I smiled and nodded my head. I could see the excitement growing on Dad's face. "And I was thinking we could move you out of the apartment and back up there where you belong."

Dad opened his mouth, then closed it before saying anything. His eyes began to tear up and he sat back in his chair. "That would make me very happy," he said.

After dinner, I dropped Dad back at his apartment and hurried home. I was anxious to tell Annie the news.

At home, I didn't even bother to take off my coat before dialing Annie's number. I sat down and closed my eyes. In my mind, red, orange and yellow oak and maple leaves framed the falls, and I could hear the sound of water rushing over and between large rocks. I inhaled, and I could smell the air saturated with an earthy, sun-soaked freshness. The imagined scene relaxed and exhilarated me as I waited for Annie to answer.

The phone rang once. I smiled and felt more contented than I had in years. It rang a second time.

"Hello," a familiar voice said.

It was good to be going home.

Back on the Road

Bird looked over the rim of his mug, and smiled. "Let's do it," he said. "We can leave right after graduation and head to Denver, just like Sal and the gang. Then we can go to San Francisco."

"You're not going to hitchhike like Kerouac did, are you?" Kyle slurred.

The familiar smell of generously salted popcorn wafted through the bar that had been a second home to us during our college lives. We had hatched one crazy idea after another in here. Like those other schemes, the "Kerouac adventure" was just supposed to be a frivolous idea, idle talk that was never meant to be taken seriously.

We were just about to graduate from college, the Class of '83. During our final semester, Kyle, Bird, and I took an American Lit class together, and one of the books we read was Jack Kerouac's *On the Road*. At the bar, after a few beers, I came up with the idea of recreating the journey the main character, Sal Paradise, made across America.

In the book, Sal is an aspiring writer who befriends Dean, a wild and undisciplined guy who has a zest for life and a penchant for living in the moment, consequences be damned. The two set out on a quest from one coast to the other in search of experience and adventure.

"We're not really being serious about this, are we?" I asked.

"Why not?" Bird asked. "It'll be great, a mad ride across Kerouac's America. Besides, what else are we going to do all summer?"

Kerouac wrote in a jazz-like style, which earned him the title, "King of the Beats," referring to his association with the Beat Generation. We really connected with his writing, and even adopted some of his odd Beat language, calling everything mad, and crazy, and hincty. Our American Lit professor told us that *On the Road* was a thinly fictionalized version of Kerouac's real life.

"I'm supposed to get a job," I said.

"You have the rest of your life to work," Bird said. "Take the summer off and see the country before you have to grow up."

He had a point. I was apprehensive about settling down into a career. I knew I'd have to do it someday, but I wasn't ready yet. "It's just a goofy idea," I said. "I wasn't being serious."

Bird refilled my beer from the plastic pitcher, then poured what was left into his own mug. A cheer went up from the people in the bar as one team or the other scored in the early-season baseball game that was on the big screen TV. We were too engrossed in our conversation to pay attention to the game.

"We should be serious," Bird said. "In less than a month we're going to be out of college, and I don't want the fun to end. It can be like our last hurrah. A farewell to our youth,"

I looked at Bird and then at Kyle. Maybe this was my way out of a life of obligation and responsibility, at least for the summer. "What do you think, Kyle?"

"We can take my car," Kyle said. "I don't want to hitchhike." Kyle's parents had bought him a new BMW M3 convertible as an early graduation gift. I was a little surprised by his answer. I had expected Kyle to crap on our plans. That was the role he usually played in our schemes.

Bird slapped Kyle on the back. "All right, Kyle." There was an excited edge to Bird's voice. "What do you say, Reno?"

I was now the only hold-out. The prospect of spending part of the summer on the road both thrilled and frightened me. I loved the idea, but worried about what my parents would say. I was also concerned about being in a car for an extended period of time with Kyle and Bird. What if the trip ruined our friendship? They were both good guys, but Kyle and Bird were very different from one another, and they tended to argue a lot.

I looked around the table. Bird was animated and wild-eyed, waiting for an answer. Kyle looked at me expectantly. "Do you really want to do this, Kyle?" I asked.

He nodded and I could see in his unfocused eyes that he was feeling the beer more than Bird or me. "Yeah, I mean, it'll be great, right?"

How could I say no? "All right," I said. "I guess we're going on a road trip.

Bird raised his hand above his head and I gave him a high five. "Lugubrious," he said.

§

My dad hadn't gone to college. He was a self-made man who had started out as a laborer for a construction company, and had gone on to own his own contracting business. He was a no-nonsense guy who viewed education as a good thing, provided it prepared you for a job. When I started college, I told him that I wanted to major in English, and eventually become a writer. He balked at this news and convinced me—mostly through guilt and parental manipulation—to major in business.

When I called home to talk to my parents about the road trip, my mom answered the phone. As soon as I told her I had some news, she had my dad get on the extension.

"Your mother says you have some news," Dad said. "I hope it's good news."

"Did you get straight A's?" Mom asked.

"No, it's not about my grades," I said. "It's about this summer."

"Did you get a job?" Dad asked.

In previous conversations, Dad had let me know that he eventually wanted me to come to work with him. He had a dream of building his contracting business into a big operation, and he harbored hopes that he and I could do that together. But first, he wanted me to get a job working somewhere else. He thought it was important that I have a year or two of real world business experience under my belt before joining him.

"No, it's not about a job either. It's about how I plan on spending the summer. I'm going to take some time and head out west for a while."

I had rehearsed what I was going to say to my parents, but it had all come out wrong. I had planned on talking about the educational nature of recreating Kerouac's journey, and how I could interview for jobs as I traveled. In the moment, I had forgotten everything I had wanted to say.

"Out west?" Mom asked.

"Yeah, just for a while," I said. "It will be a good opportunity to unwind a little before—"

"I don't think that's a very good idea, Son," Dad said. "Businesses are hiring college graduates now, not at the end of the summer."

"Well, what I thought was—"

"You know, I didn't pay for you to go to college just so you could go on some foolish road trip. You're twenty-two years old now. It's time to buckle down and get on with life. College is over."

"Was this Bird's idea?" Mom asked.

Neither Mom nor Dad particularly liked Bird. Two years earlier, they had come to town for a visit, and had witnessed Bird running down the hall of our dorm wearing nothing but his underwear and a pair of sunglasses.

My parents were afraid that Bird would somehow lead me astray. He had been raised by a single mother who didn't set many limits on him, which really bothered my parents. I also think that, because Bird came from a fairly poor upbringing, they were afraid he would try to take financial advantage of me. They never said that in so many words, but the implication was always there.

"Bird and Kyle are going with me," I said, "but it wasn't Bird's idea. It was mine."

"Kyle's parents are letting him go?" Dad asked.

"Yeah, they said it's okay," I said, although the truth was that I didn't know if Kyle had even talked to his parents.

Mom and Dad were quiet for a moment. My hope was that invoking Kyle's parents' permission would sway my parents' opinion about the trip. Kyle's family owned a bank, and they were very well off financially. Because of this, my parents looked up to them, and gave their opinions undo respect. Kyle's parents were fine, but it bugged me that my parent's sentiment toward them was based primarily on the size of their bank account.

They also liked Kyle because he was frugal with his money—some would say cheap—and he and his girlfriend, Joan, were in a long-term relationship, something my parents wanted for me. At times, I thought they'd prefer that Kyle was their son.

"Steven, you're old enough to make your own decisions," Dad said. "I don't like the idea. I think you'd be better off putting this kind of nonsense behind you, and getting on with your life. But if you want to go, I'm not going to tell you that you can't."

I hated the feeling of having to get my parents' blessing. My dad was right: I was old enough to make my own decisions. Even so, I was still financially dependent on my parents, and I knew they held certain expectations of me, expectations I didn't like, but felt an obligation to meet.

I breathed a sigh of relief. It wasn't exactly an unreserved blessing, but it was good enough. Getting past my parents' objections was going to be the biggest hurdle I had to overcome. The trip was on, and now the fun could begin.

§

We were on the road for three days before we hit Denver, the first stop on our adventure that had anything to do with Kerouac's book. Dean was from there, and during Sal's first trip west, he had hitchhiked to Denver to meet up with Dean and his other friends. Denver played a big role in the book and in Kerouac's life, so we decided to spend a couple of days there.

On our first night in town we went down to Larimer Street, Denver's skid row, where Dean's wino father did his drinking in *On the Road*. The area was going through a change. Old buildings were being torn down and new ones were being built. Shiny new skyscrapers stood alongside boarded up two and three story buildings. You could see that the old buildings, despite being in disrepair, had once been show places, with arched windows, fancy facades, and other decorative touches. It didn't look like much now, but I could imagine how Larimer Street must have looked fifty or seventy-five years earlier.

Kyle pulled the car up to the curb in front of a place called Howie's Tap Room. A man sat on the sidewalk in front of a boarded up building next door, drinking from a brown paper bag.

We went into Howie's, sat down at the bar, and each ordered a Coors. We had a reverence for Coors because the brewery didn't ship their beer east of the Mississippi. During our college years, we had made several trips across the river from Illinois into Iowa to score the hard-to-get brew with the label that indicated it was a "banquet beer." We had no idea what that meant, but it seemed to add to the allure of drinking it.

We were sitting on round-topped bar stools with rotating seats covered in green faux leather. The seats were ripped and worn, and they squeaked when they were turned. Two other guys sat at the bar with us. There was a couple huddled together at a table in the corner, and four guys at another table across the barroom talking loudly and laughing. The air was hazy in the dimly lit bar and it smelled of stale beer and tobacco smoke.

Bird swiveled around on his bar stool and looked at the barroom. "Just think, Jack Kerouac could have drank right here in this bar. Hell, he might have sat right on this bar stool."

"He could have," I said. "I think the stools might be that old."

"Did you guys really like the book that much?" Kyle asked. "I thought it was kind of boring, and the language Kerouac used was weird. I mean words like 'hincty' and how Dean always said, 'He knows time.' Even that goofy word Bird is always using."

"What word?" Bird asked.

"Lugubrious. I'm not sure what it means, but I'm pretty sure you use it wrong."

"Lugubrious? That's a great word," Bird said.

"What *does* it mean?" I asked. "Do you know?"

Bird took a long pull from his beer then set the bottle on the bar. "No, but it's a great word."

"You guys ready for another one?" the bartender asked.

I told him we wanted another round of "The Banquet Beer" and he walked to the other end of the bar where the cooler was.

"You boys out slumming tonight?" asked a gravelly voice from behind us. I turned on my bar stool and saw a man with shaggy brown hair and an unkempt beard. He was wearing a threadbare yellow t-shirt and dirty jeans with a hole in the right knee.

"We're just having a beer," I said, feeling like one of us should say something.

"Don't they have bars out where you live?" the bearded man asked. "Maybe you should go back home to Mommy and Daddy. This ain't no place for some weak-assed college boys."

Bird stood up from his bar stool, but before he could do anything, the bartender said, "Leave them alone, Dale. I don't want you causing any shit in here tonight."

Dale was unsteady on his feet. He stared at the bartender for a moment and then walked toward the back of the bar, where the bathrooms were. "Bunch of college pussies," he muttered.

"What's his problem?" Kyle asked the bartender, who had returned with our beers.

"He's just drunk," the bartender said.

Bird watched Dale walk toward the bathrooms and then he sat back on his barstool.

"Let's finish these beers and then head somewhere else." I raised my bottle in a toast. We each tilted our beers back.

When Dale returned from the bathroom he had a cigarette dangling from his lip. I expected him to say something, but he just walked by silently and rejoined his friends.

We left Howie's, and walked past the boarded up building next door. The wino still sat on the sidewalk, brown paper bag in hand. A few doors down we went into a bar called The Ginn Mill, a place we hoped had been around when Kerouac had prowled the area. We wanted to connect our visit to Larimer Street to the writer and his book.

The barroom at The Ginn Mill was long and narrow, with the bar on the right and tables against the brick wall on the left. The bar was rounded on the end nearest the front door, and the wood, which must have once been stained and lustrous, was worn and in need of varnish. My eye was drawn up to the intricate copper ceiling, which had dulled over the years. The place wasn't very fancy now, but I could tell that it had been at one time.

We sat down at the bar. Although the barstools had seats covered in faux leather just like Howie's, these barstools were affixed to the floor and didn't move. They were not particularly comfortable.

There were more people at The Ginn Mill than there had been at Howie's, and the atmosphere seemed to be more upbeat. There were two bartenders, a guy with a full beard wearing a vest over his stripped shirt, and a woman with short, dark hair and what looked to be a perpetual smile. The female bartender came down to our end of the bar.

We ordered a round of Coors, and when she brought them, Bird asked, "Do you know if Jack Kerouac ever came in here to drink?"

The bartender's eyes flashed. "Is that why you guys are here? To find the ghost of the late, great Jack Kerouac?"

"We just wondered if he used to drink here," Bird said, "but if his ghost is here, we'd like to see it."

The bartender laughed. "Sorry boys, there's no ghost. But rumor has it he did drink here once or twice with his crazy friend Neal Cassady."

"Cassady was the guy that Kerouac based Dean Moriarty on," Kyle said.

"That's right. In other books, Kerouac called him Cody Pomeray," she said.

"How do you know so much?" Bird asked.

"Because I'm smart," she said. "And because I'm getting a Masters in Lit at CU Denver." The bartender introduced herself as Carlene.

"CU Denver?" I asked.

"It's the Denver campus of the University of Colorado. Where are you guys from?"

We told her and explained why we were visiting Larimer Street.

"I've never understood why *On the Road* is so damned popular," she said. "It's one of Kerouac's worst books. Both *Dharma Bums* and *Big Sur* are better. Have you read them?"

Although I was more of a reader than either Kyle or Bird, I had read neither, and had never even heard of *Big Sur*. We all admitted we hadn't read either book.

"If you're really interested in Kerouac, you should read them," Carlene said. "He hung around this area, but I think he hung around Five Points even more."

"Where's that?" I asked.

"It's up Larimer Street about eight or ten blocks north of here. If you go up there, you should check out a place called the Crystal Grill Tavern. They've got a great cheeseburger. Greasy, but really good."

We finished our beers and headed out to the car. We hadn't eaten dinner, and a greasy burger sounded good. We were just about to the car when our old buddy Dale came staggering out of Howie's with another guy.

"Hey look," Dale said. "The pussies are back."

Kyle was standing the closest to Dale and said, "We don't want any—"

Before Kyle could get his hands out of his pockets, Dale hit him square in the face with an awkward punch. Kyle's knees buckled and he went down. Dale leaned over Kyle, apparently waiting for him to get up and fight. Bird grabbed Dale by the shoulder, turned him around, and let loose with a ferocious kick to his groin. Dale grabbed his crotch and teetered to the side, falling in a heap. He lay on the sidewalk holding himself, and moaning loudly.

"Hey," Dale's friend yelled, looking down at his crumpled compatriot. I pushed him away from Kyle, and he tripped, tumbling over Dale.

I turned and saw Bird helping Kyle up. "Are you okay?" I asked Kyle.

"Yeah, let's just get out of here," Kyle said, opening the driver's door. Bird climbed in the back and I got into the front passenger seat. Dale and his buddy were still lying on the sidewalk when we pulled away from the curb and headed north up Larimer.

§

The Crystal Grill was in a squat, rundown brick building with a back-lighted 7-Up sign over the door and a couple of "Schlitz" signs on the front wall. We walked in and immediately felt out of place. We were the only white people in the joint. Kyle turned to walk back outside, but Bird marched past him and sat down at the bar. Kyle and I joined him.

"Three Coors, and we'd like to see some menus," Bird said.

The bartender nodded and walked away.

The bar was smoky and had the smell of beer and charred meat mixed with tobacco smoke. I thought I smelled marijuana as well. Marvin Gay sang "Sexual Healing" on the juke box.

"Maybe we should leave," Kyle said. His eye was beginning to swell from Dale's punch.

"Because of your eye?" Bird asked. "I thought you were hungry?"

Kyle looked around the barroom. "No, it's not my eye. I don't think this is a place for white people."

"You worry too much," Bird said.

"I trust you boys are all of legal drinking age?" the bartender said.

"We are."

The bartender set a beer in front of each of us and then reached under the bar and brought out three menus.

"Is it okay that we're in here?" Kyle had his hand up to his mouth and spoke to the bartender in a hushed, conspiratorial tone. He looked over his shoulder at the other people in the barroom.

"Why wouldn't it be?" the bartender asked, a perplexed look on his face.

"You know, because we're white," Kyle said, still keeping his voice low.

"I hadn't noticed," the bartender said. "Let me ask you this: what color is your money?"

"Green," I said.

"That's the only color I'm worried about. As long as your money is green, you can come in here, and nobody going to bother you."

Kyle let out a nervous laugh and nodded. "Okay. Good. Thanks."

"What would you like to eat?" the bartender asked.

We each ordered a cheeseburger and fries.

"Three cheeseburgers and three orders of fries," the bartender said, then walked back to the kitchen.

"Why would you ask a question like that?" Bird asked Kyle.

"What? I just wanted to make sure we were welcome."

"Don't you think it's kind of insulting?"

"No," Kyle said. "I think it's better to know."

"It is a little insulting," I said. "Why would you assume that they don't want us in here just because we're white?"

"I don't know. I didn't mean anything by it."

The bartender rejoined us. "What happened to your eye?"

Kyle reached up and touched his quickly swelling eye. "I got hit."

"I hope the other guy looks worse."

"He was still lying on the sidewalk last time we saw him," Bird said.

"Is that right?" The bartender said. He walked away, then came back with a bag of frozen onion rings. "Put this on your eye. It'll keep the swelling down."

Kyle took the bag and placed it against his face. "Thanks."

"You ready for another beer?"

"I am," Bird said.

"How about you guys?" the bartender asked.

I said I was ready for another one and Kyle nodded, although his beer was still half full.

The burgers came out and were as good as Carlene promised, greasy and delicious. We devoured them in silence, too busy to talk.

When we finished, Kyle suggested we order another round of Coors. He was apparently feeling more comfortable after the burger and a few beers. When "Midnight Train to Georgia" came on the juke box, he started to sing along. Bird and I joined in. We let Gladys Knight sing lead and we sang along with the Pips, something we had done often at the bar we hung out at in college. As Gladys sang, we pivoted in unison on our bar stools, turning to the right and reaching out with our left arms, then pivoting to the left and reaching out with our right arms. When Gladys sang the chorus, we each reached up in the air as if we were pulling a train whistle and sang, "whoo, whoo."

When the song ended, a group of five or six people that were sitting in a booth behind us applauded. The bartender was smiling and clapping.

§

In *On The Road*, Sal and some of his pals leave Denver and head into the mountains. In Central City, Sal attends the world famous Opera House, where he sees "Fidelio." The gang has a great time barhopping and throwing a party in an old miner's shack. But by the end of the night, everyone gets too drunk, fights break out, and the party breaks up. The next morning, when Sal and his friends head back to Denver, they feel defeated and depressed. We skipped the opera and the good times, and went straight to the depression.

Central City wasn't what we thought it would be. We expected a thriving old west mining town with bars and restaurants and a lot going on. Instead, what we found was a dusty, worn-out town with dilapidated, boarded up buildings, and signs posted all over concerning hazardous waste left behind from silver mining. The area had recently been designated an EPA Superfund site.

The opera house was still in operation, but we weren't interested in attending. There were a few bars and restaurants, but it didn't look like anything much was going on. The town was quiet, and the people we saw vanished into the shadows of rundown buildings so quickly we weren't sure we'd seen them at all. We parked on the curb, and wandered around the downtown area.

"This sure doesn't seem like the place old Jack described in the book," I said.

"Yeah, it looks like they've fallen on hard times since Kerouac was here," Kyle said.

Bird looked around at the neglected buildings and the sad town. "Let's find a bar. I could use a drink."

Down the street from where we had parked was a bar called The Gold Coin Saloon. It was located in a crumbling, uninviting brick building. We had to walk through swinging saloon doors to enter, and when we got inside, a guy wearing a torn Denver Broncos jersey was walking backwards toward the doors.

"Come on, Sam. I can pay you next week," the man said.

"I told you," the bartender said, "don't come back in here unless you have money." The bartender held a baseball bat.

I had to move out of the way so the man backing out of the door didn't run into me. He left, and we walked up to the bar and sat down on barstools with hard, wooden tops.

The bartender walked behind the bar to greet us. "What can I get for you?" He was still holding the bat and looked pissed.

"Three Coors," I said, trying to sound like a guy who didn't want to make any trouble.

"Why do you want to drink that skunk water when there's decent beer to be had?" The bartender had a gruff, Nick Nolte-like voice.

We looked at each other, not sure how to respond. "You don't like Coors?" Bird finally asked.

"No I don't. I'm a Budweiser man."

We looked at each other again, then back at the bartender, but nobody spoke.

"Hell, if you like it, then drink it," he said. "I'm just trying to be friendly."

Bird nodded. "Okay then, three Coors."

The bartender shook his head, and, after storing the baseball bat under the bar, poured three Coors from the tap. It was the middle of the afternoon and we were the only customers in the place. The wooden bar was worn from years of use, and the plaster walls were cracked and dull, but the barroom had a historic quality I liked. It looked like this place actually could have been around back in the Wild West days.

The bartender set a beer in front of each of us and then walked away without saying a word.

"What crawled up his ass?" Kyle asked.

"You wouldn't be too happy either if you had to live here," Bird said.

When the bartender walked back toward us, we stopped talking and drank our beers. He poured a Budweiser from the tap into a tall clear glass and drank down half of it. "Ah, that's good beer," he said to no one in particular. He then turned his attention to us. "What brings you to Central City?"

"We came up here hoping to see anything related to Jack Kerouac," I said.

"Why would you want to come up into the mountains for that hack of a writer? You must have read *On the Road*."

"We did. Don't you like Kerouac?"

"I think he sucked, although *Dharma Bums* wasn't all bad. That sniveling little twit came up here for one night, got drunk, got into a fight, then went home and wrote about it like he was the king of Central City. I don't think he's nothing but a poser and a wannabe. I hate all that beatnik shit." The bartender had both of his hands on the bar and was leaning over it toward us.

"Other than that, Missus Lincoln, how did you like the play?" I said.

The bartender stared at me for a second, then got a smile on his face. He leaned back away from the bar and pointed at me. "That's pretty funny. You boys just earned yourself a free drink." He explained that his name was Smilin' Sam Ridley, and customers who could make him smile got a drink on the house. Few ever collected, and he seemed impressed that we had gotten him to smile. "I reckon you won't be able to do it again during your visit," he said.

We finished our beers and Sam brought fresh ones. "Do you really hate Kerouac as much as you say?" Kyle asked.

"I think he's a shitty writer, and he's the last person I'd come to the mountains for. There are so many other more important people who have visited town."

"Like who?"

"Doc Holliday and Buffalo Bill Cody both drank right here in the Gold Coin," Sam said, pounding his index finger against the top of the wooden bar. "President Ulysses S. Grant came to town two different times. Hell, you want a writer, Mark Twain came to Central City, and he was a damn sight better than Kerouac."

I tilted my bottle of Coors back, not sure how to respond to what Sam had said.

"Is that miner's shack where Kerouac stayed still standing?" Bird asked.

Sam let out sigh. "You're really not listening, are you? No, the shack is gone. Now enough talk about that goddamn Jack Kerouac. I feel like telling a joke." He walked over to the tap, re-filled his glass, and came back to stand in front of us.

"An old man walks into a pub in Scotland, shuffles across the floor, and sits down at the bar. In a sad, defeated voice he orders a beer. The bartender draughts a mug for him and asks why he looks so down in the dumps." Sam took a drink from his beer, and seemed to be getting into character.

"Ah, I tell you, man," he said with a Scottish accent, "look out that window there. You see that fence. I built that fence with me own two hands. But do they call me McGregor the fence builder? No. And that bridge across the burn? I built that bridge with the sweat of me brow, but do they call me McGregor the bridge builder. No they do not."

Sam rubbed the bar in front of him. "And this bar, I built it from the finest wild cherry wood available in all the land. But do they call me McGregor the bar builder? No they don't. But you fuck one lousy goat..."

We all laughed, but Sam stayed stone-faced, just drinking his beer.

§

Driving the Vegas strip to our hotel felt like what I imagined an acid flashback would feel like. Buildings, marquees, and billboards were all lit up with bright, flashing neon lights. The beeping horns and spastic brake lights of stop-and-go traffic added to the garish quality of the glittering, glaring city. I liked the idea of doing a little gambling, but I found Las Vegas breathtakingly gaudy. I looked forward to leaving almost as soon as we arrived.

When we got to our hotel room, the first thing Bird wanted to do was visit the Chicken Ranch, a whorehouse about an hour outside the city. He had been talking about getting a hooker ever since we started our trip five days earlier. Kyle was tired of listening to Bird's plan to pay for sex.

"What's the big deal?" Bird asked. "It's legal there."

"I don't care if it is legal," Kyle said. "I'm not going to a whorehouse. Do you know what my parents would do to me if they found out? Joan would cut off my balls."

"Are you sure she hasn't done that already?" Bird asked.

"Very funny," Kyle said. "What do you think, Reno?"

Bird had an innocent, hopeful look on his face. "If you're so hell-bent on getting a hooker, why don't you just find one here at the hotel?" I asked. "I'm sure there must be some hanging around."

"But it's not legal here," Bird said.

"Do you really care?"

Bird tilted his head back and stared at the ceiling. After a moment, he began to smile. "No, I guess not."

"So we're not going to the Chicken Ranch, right?" Kyle asked.

"Nope. You and I can gamble while Bird looks for a hooker."

Kyle nodded his head. "For God's sake, Bird, don't get caught."

"Don't worry, Kyle. Your balls are safe."

Kyle laughed. "Thanks. That's very reassuring."

On the casino floor, the bell and whistle sounds of slot machines mixed with the indistinguishable murmur of people gasping and celebrating and laughing. Smoke rose from the gaming tables toward the brightly lit ceiling, and scantily clad waitresses in sequined outfits delivered colorful drinks to thirsty gamblers. It was an orgy for the senses.

We agreed that no one would risk more than one hundred dollars. Kyle made a beeline for the nickel slots, and Bird and I headed to the blackjack table. Bird stood behind me at the table while I played. I encouraged him to sit down and join the game, but he said he just wanted to watch.

I started out hot, winning the first three hands. It felt good watching my stack of chips grow. I had some back-and-forth luck, but during the course of the next few hours, my stack got bigger and bigger. I didn't notice that, at some point, Bird had wandered off.

After almost three hours playing blackjack, my luck started to run out, so I took my chips and left the table. I found Kyle at the same slot machine where we had left him.

"I'm up eight dollars and thirty cents." Kyle spoke with so much excitement it sounded like he was up thousands of dollars.

"That's great."

"How did you do?" he asked.

"I haven't counted it yet," I said, "but I did pretty good. Do you want to go get something to eat?"

Kyle stared at the lever of the slot machine. "I don't know," he said. "I'm hot right now."

"You can always come back."

He looked at me, but didn't answer. The swelling was gone, but he still had a slightly black eye.

"They have an all-you-can-eat buffet for just five bucks," I said.

"I am kind of hungry," he said. "I can pay for it out of my winnings and still have money left over."

"Right," I said, amused. "I just need to cash in these chips."

When we got up to the cashier's window, a woman with jet black hair asked how she could help us. Her hair was pulled back tight and she wore it in a long, thick pony-tail.

I put the cup with my chips in it down on the counter and slid it towards her. "I'd like to cash out, please." I felt nervous. Vegas made me uneasy.

The cashier counted the chips quickly, reached into her drawer, and counted out the cash as she laid it down in front of me. "One hundred, two hundred, three hundred, four hundred, five hundred, five fifty, five seventy, five hundred and seventy five dollars."

"Holy crap!" Kyle said, remembering that I had started with one hundred bucks. "You won four hundred and seventy-five dollars?"

"Yeah, I guess I did," I said, a little surprised myself. Kyle let out a "whoop" and patted me on the back.

I looked at the cashier. She was used to doling out big money to high rollers, and was amused by Kyle's excitement. "Congratulations," she said. She had a big smile, with perfect teeth that looked to be capped.

"Yeah, thanks." I folded the money and put it into my pocket. "I guess I'm buying," I said to Kyle.

§

We walked out of the restaurant after we finished eating and were assaulted by the bright lights and the cacophony of casino sounds.

"God, did you know it's already one-thirty in the morning?" Kyle asked. "We should probably call it a night. We're leaving for Rancho in a few hours."

Just then, a large man with close cropped hair approached us. He was wearing a brown sport coat with a darker brown turtle neck underneath. "Are you Steve Roberts?" he asked. I noticed that the sleeves of his sport coat were straining because of the size of his arms.

"Yeah, that's me," I said.

"Could you come with me, sir?" What Brown Sport Coat said was phrased as a question, but it sounded like there was only one right answer.

"Why? What's going on?" I asked. Either I had inadvertently cheated at blackjack, or this guy was going to steal my money.

"Your friend Brad is in a little trouble," Brown Sport Coat said. "He said you might be able to help him."

It took me a second to remember that "Brad" was Bird's real name. "Trouble? What kind of trouble?"

"It's probably best if we just go up to your room to discuss this," he said. Brown Sport Coat had been extremely polite, which for some odd reason made me trust him.

"Sure," I said. As if I had a choice.

When we got up to the room, Bird was sitting on an unmade bed in his underwear. The blanket was on the floor and the sheets were rumpled. A large man in a blue sport coat stood next to the bed and a woman in a slinky cocktail dress sat on the couch, smoking a cigarette.

"Hey, guys," Bird said. He tried to stand up, but Blue Sport Coat pushed him back down on the bed.

"What's going on?" I asked.

Brown Sport Coat closed the door behind us and turned his attention to me. "Your friend here employed this young lady," he said, gesturing to the only woman in the room, "for her services this evening, but when it was time to pay, he didn't have enough money."

"I thought she said a hundred dollars," Bird said. He shrugged and held out his hands.

"A hundred dollars? Do I look like a hundred-dollar hooker to you?" the woman asked. Her voice was loud and she seemed more insulted than angry. She wore a low-cut, shiny silver dress that accentuated her impressive, freckled cleavage. Her auburn hair was thick and curled. I didn't have any experience with hookers, but she didn't look like a hundred-dollar hooker to me. She was poised and fit, and her movements were elegant and graceful.

"Let's all keep our voices down," Brown Sport Coat said. "People are trying to sleep."

"What does he owe you?" I asked the woman. The way her dress glittered in the light mesmerized me. I couldn't keep my eyes off of her.

"Your friend owes the young lady four hundred dollars," Brown Sport Coat said.

"You paid four hundred dollars to get laid?" Kyle asked.

Bird smiled and shrugged.

"Please, keep your voice down," Brown Sport Coat said to Kyle. He turned toward me. "If you could just pay the young lady, we could forget this ever happened."

The mention of paying the beautiful woman snapped me out of the trance I had been under since first laying eyes on Bird's "date" for the evening. "Four hundred dollars. That didn't last long," I said half under my breath. I reached into my pocket for the money, peeled off four one-hundred-dollar bills, and handed them to Brown Sport Coat. For some reason, I didn't want to hand them to the woman.

"Thank you, gentlemen," Brown Sport Coat said. "Have a good evening."

The woman stood. I was staring again, and she noticed. She walked over to me, and gave me a soft kiss that barely brushed my lips. I thought my knees were going to buckle.

"Thank you," she said, her voice low and sexy.

"Hey, don't I get a good night kiss?" Bird asked.

The woman glared at Bird for a moment, then she and her large friends left the room.

When the door closed, Kyle and I both looked at Bird, who was still sitting on the bed in his underwear.

"What? For four hundred dollars I don't even get a good night kiss?" he said.

"Bird," Kyle said, "you're going to end up getting us killed."

"I got the kiss because it was my money." I tried to sound angry. "I just won that four hundred dollars and I expect you to—" I burst out laughing. The situation was just too funny. I wanted to be mad at Bird, but I couldn't. Bird started laughing too.

"Fine, you guys can laugh if you want," Kyle said, "but I don't think it's funny. I'm going to bed."

The next morning, Kyle was still angry. I convinced Bird to apologize to him, although he didn't see what he had done wrong.

"Hey Kyle," Bird said. "Sorry about last night." He sounded sincere to me, but I knew him well enough to doubt that he was. He was simply doing what I had asked.

"Was it worth four hundred dollars?" Kyle snapped.

"Yeah, it was," Bird said, as if Kyle really expected an answer. I couldn't help but laugh. Bird wasn't joking. He really thought it had been worth four hundred dollars, especially since the money hadn't come out of his pocket.

"Just forget it," Kyle said, shaking his head. "Let's get going."

I think we'd all had enough of Las Vegas.

§

We left town a little before noon and headed southwest down I-15 toward Rancho Cucamonga, near Los Angeles, where Kyle's friend Ed lived. They hadn't seen each other for about a year, but had kept in touch through letters and phone calls.

Ed was a couple of years older than us, and although I'd never met him, I felt like I knew him because Kyle talked about him so much. I was grateful he was letting us crash at his place while we were in town.

There wasn't much to look at as we crossed the desert from Nevada into California. We had the radio on and we were singing a Duran Duran song, "Hungry Like the Wolf," as loud as we could.

Kyle seemed to have forgiven Bird for his indiscretion the previous night. He was singing along with the rest of us, bouncing around in his seat, and pounding out the beat on the steering wheel.

"I'm looking forward to seeing Ed," Kyle said when the song had ended. "He's a really great guy. I think you guys are going to like him.

"How do you know Ed?" Bird asked.

"His dad and my dad have known each other for years. Our families used to get together when we were young, and Ed and I became friends. We used to be life guards together up at camp in Wisconsin. He's almost like a big brother to me."

"Why did he move to California," I asked.

"He got a job at an investment firm. He's been out here for more than two years. He might be making over six figures now."

"But is he happy?" Bird asked.

"With that kind of money, who wouldn't be?" Kyle asked.

In Barstow, we stopped for gas. Kyle got in the back seat to take a nap. Bird was sitting in the passenger seat with his shoes off and his feet up on the dash. I took the wheel.

Near the Oak Hill Road exit on I-15 we saw a woman on the side of the road with her thumb out. She wore a red and white checked top and a pair of cut-off jean shorts. As we approached, we saw that she had kinky blond hair, and she carried a backpack.

"Pull over," Bird said. "We've got to pick her up." I expected Kyle to protest, but he was fast asleep. I slowed and pulled over to the side of the road about fifty yards in front of her.

"Kyle, wake up." I reached into the back seat and shook him awake.

"What? What's wrong?"

"Nothing," Bird said, "but we're going to have another passenger."

Kyle was confused until the back door opened and the blonde climbed in next to him.

"Hi," she said. "Thanks for stopping." She had a voice that was smoky and sexy and dreamy.

"No problem," Bird said. "We're happy to help."

We introduced ourselves and found out that our new friend was named Candy. She was going to Rancho Cucamonga, where she was supposed to meet a friend.

"We're going to Rancho, too," I said. "We can take you all the way there."

We drove for about 20 minutes. Bird was trying his best to get Candy's attention, but she seemed to have more of an interest in Kyle. As they talked, Candy put her hand on Kyle's leg. At one point, she put her arms around his neck, and leaned her head on his shoulder in a sort of hug.

Candy was just over five feet tall with tanned skin and bright white teeth that flashed whenever she smiled, which she did a lot. I kept looking in the rearview mirror at her. Bird was turned around in his seat and Kyle was just as attentive as he could be.

Candy asked where we would be staying in Rancho, and we told her about Kyle's friend, Ed. She said she didn't live in town, but knew a lot of people in the area. She wanted to know where he worked, where he lived, and what he looked like. It never was clear where Candy lived, although it seemed she didn't know Ed.

We exited I-15 at Foothill Boulevard and drove west into town. After a few miles, Candy asked me to turn left onto Archibald Avenue. Almost as soon as we turned, she pointed to a parking lot and said, "Pull in there."

Bird was trying to find out what Candy would be doing later that evening, but Candy suddenly seemed uninterested. She grabbed the neck of her shirt and ripped it open so her white bra was showing. We all just stared without saying a word.

"Okay guys, here's the deal," she said. "See the woman up there by the door of that shop? That's my friend. If I'm not out of the car in one minute, she's going to call the cops and report an attempted rape. She knows what your car looks like and she has your license number."

"What the hell do you want?" I asked.

"I want you to give me all of your cash. Hurry up and don't hold out. Give it all to me."

Kyle dug deep into his pocket and pulled out all of his money. Candy took it and put it into her backpack. "Now you two," she said to Bird and me. She was all business. We hesitated, and she screamed at us, "Hurry up. I'm not playing around with you."

"Just give her the money," Kyle said.

I reached into my pocket and pulled out all of the cash I had. Bird did the same thing. I took his money and handed it all to Candy. She stuffed the money into her backpack and opened the car door.

"Thanks for the ride, guys," she said. "Now I want you to pull out of here and don't come back." She slammed the door and walked quickly toward her friend.

"Let's get the hell out of here before she calls the cops," Kyle said.

"She's not going to call the cops," Bird said. "She just robbed us. She doesn't want the cops around."

"Do you want to take that chance?" Kyle said. "Let's get out of here."

I pulled out of the parking lot going south on Archibald.

"Turn right here and stop," Bird said.

"Why?" Kyle asked in a panic.

"Just do it, Reno. Trust me."

I turned right onto Hampshire Street and stopped. Bird quickly opened the door. "Go around the block, and then come back here to get me."

"What are you doing?" Kyle shouted, but Bird had already closed the door and was running back toward the parking lot where we had left Candy.

We drove through a residential neighborhood. It seemed to take forever before I came to a street that turned to the right so I could go back and get Bird. I turned on Malachite Avenue and took it back to Foothill Boulevard. The afternoon traffic was busy and I had a hard time pulling out onto the street. Finally, I forced my way into traffic. Car horns blared and tires squealed as I drove quickly back to Archibald. I took a right and floored the car down to Hampshire. Bird was waiting at the corner.

"What did you do?" Kyle demanded.

"I wanted to see if I could catch a glimpse of Candy's friend or the car they were driving," Bird said. He was breathing hard from running.

"What did you see?" I asked.

"I got a good look at Candy's friend. She's tall, like almost six feet tall. She has long dark hair. Maybe black or dark brown."

"Did they see you?" Kyle asked, a mixture of anger and fear in his voice.

"No," Bird said, "but I saw their car and I got their license plate number." Bird smiled, looking proud of himself.

"So what?" Kyle asked. "What are you going to do with that information? You can't call the cops."

"Why not?" Bird asked, turning around in his seat to face Kyle. "They ripped us off. We didn't do anything wrong."

"But the cops don't know that," Kyle said. "Who are they going to believe? Cute little Candy with the ripped shirt or the three horny guys from Illinois?"

"That's not how—" Bird started to say.

"Forget it," Kyle said. "We're not going to call the cops. I'm not going to try to explain why we picked a woman up off the side of the road or how Candy's top got ripped. No one is going to believe us. Let's just go find Ed and forget about this."

Bird turned toward me. "Reno, shouldn't we call the cops?"

I was in the middle again. In theory, Bird was right about Candy ripping us off. I respected his ability to analyze a situation quickly and sort it out. He had a confidence in himself and his opinions that I admired. Even so, I was afraid that in this situation, Kyle was right.

"I don't know, Bird," I said. "I'd like to get back at her, but I think I have to agree with Kyle. We'd have a hard time convincing the cops that we're the victims."

Bird sat back in his seat and hit the door with his fist. "I can't believe you guys."

We drove to Ed's office in silence, and when we got there, Kyle went inside. Bird and I stayed in the car.

"Why didn't you want to call the cops?" Bird asked. "If we would have called right away, maybe they would have been able to catch her. Now she's long gone."

"I know," I said. "I just don't think the California cops are going to take too kindly to some out-of-state punks coming into their town causing trouble."

"But we didn't do anything wrong."

"I know, but I'm not sure we could convince them of that."

I was quiet for a few minutes until Kyle returned to the car. I could see from the look on his face that there was a problem.

"What's wrong?" I asked as Kyle got into the car.

Kyle was shaking his head. "I don't know. They said that Ed doesn't work there. He used to, but he quit about four months ago."

"He didn't tell you?" I asked.

"That's the weird thing. I talked to him just a week ago and he didn't say a word." Kyle was still shaking his head in disbelief. "I have his home address. Let's go find him."

We went to a nearby gas station and got directions to Ed's apartment. He lived on the second floor of an older two-story house. A gutter hung down on one side of the house, and the small yard was overgrown with long grass and weeds.

"This isn't the kind of place I pictured Ed living in," Kyle said, knocking on the weathered door. There was no answer.

"Can I help you?" an elderly man asked as he walked around the side of the house. We told him that we were looking for Ed. "Oh, you must be his friends from Illinois. I'm his landlord. I live downstairs." The man took an old, yellowed handkerchief out of his back pocket and blew his nose. He looked at the handkerchief, refolded it, then put it back in his pocket. "Ed's working right now. He won't be home until after nine tonight."

"Working?" Kyle asked. "Where does he work?"

"At a jewelry store over on Calle Bresca." The old man gave us directions to the store and we were once again off in search of the elusive Ed.

Inside the jewelry store, we walked past two short glass cases, one to our left and one to our right. The store was brightly lit, and the cases held what looked to be expensive watches, necklaces, and rings. A pale, older woman with dark curly hair stood behind a long glass case directly in front of us. She smiled and asked how she could help us. When Kyle told her that we were looking for Ed, she went into a back room and came out with a security guard.

"Ed?" Kyle asked.

"Kyle, you made it." Ed was dressed in a full black uniform, polished black dress shoes, and a black cap with an embroidered gold star on it. On his uniform he wore a metal badge. Patches on his shoulders indicated he worked for Ultimate Security Forces. He had a gun on his right hip.

"I thought you were a financial analyst," Kyle said.

"It's a long story," Ed said, motioning to his uniform. "I'll tell you about it later." Kyle introduced us to Ed, and we all shook hands.

"I don't get off work until nine," Ed said. "Do you think you guys can hang out until then? I can give you the key to my apartment if you want to stay there."

We left the jewelry store and went back to Ed's apartment. I wandered around the place, and found clothes strewn over most of the furniture in the living room, and dishes piled up in the sink of the small kitchen. A bedroom immediately off the living room had an unmade bed, and there were more clothes on the floor. The tiny bathroom was outdated with faded yellow tile on the walls and an old-style pedestal sink. The curtain around the bathtub was pulled back and there was a visible ring of dirt around the inside of the tub.

We were exhausted, and each found a place to take a nap. Bird lay on top of the blankets in Ed's unmade bed, Kyle spread out on an outdated couch, and I fell asleep in the faux-leather recliner.

We had been sleeping for a couple of hours when Ed's phone rang. Kyle answered it on the second ring, then asked if we wanted to meet Ed at a local bar after he got off work.

"As long as he's buying," I said. "We don't have any money."

"I have sixty dollars," Bird said. He pulled three twenties out of his pocket."

"You held out on Candy?" I asked.

"I wasn't going to give her *all* of my money."

Kyle told Ed we'd meet him at the bar. When he hung up the phone, he let out a long sigh. "I don't know what's going on with Ed." he said.

"What do you mean?" Bird asked.

"He came out to California for a good job, and now he's living in this place and working as a security guard. It's like I don't know him anymore."

"Maybe he got shit-canned for stealing money," Bird said. "You should ask him about it."

"Ed didn't steal any money," Kyle said.

"How do you know?" Bird asked. "People change."

"I don't know what's going on with him, but I'm going to find out," Kyle said. He stood from the couch and looked around the disheveled apartment. "Let's go."

§

We pulled into the parking lot, and saw Ed, still in his security guard uniform, leaning against the front of his car. We all walked across the parking lot towards the bar when Bird began jumping up and down, pointing at a car near the entrance to the bar. "That's it!" he said. "That's their car."

"What are you yelling about?" Kyle asked.

"That car right there." Bird pointed again. "That's Candy's car."

"Who's Candy?" Ed asked.

"It's a long story," Kyle said. "We probably shouldn't go in there."

"Are you kidding?" Bird said. "This is our chance to get our money back."

"No way. You're going to get us arrested," Kyle said.

"Arrested?" Ed said. "Will somebody please tell me what's going on?"

"We didn't do anything wrong," Bird said. "We're not going to get arrested. And Candy isn't going to want to involve the cops. We're going to get our money back, and our policeman friend here is going to help us." Bird put his arm around Ed's shoulder.

"What the hell is going on?" Ed asked, yet again.

We told Ed what had happened earlier in the day, and Bird explained his plan, which involved us going in to confront Candy while Ed stood by the door in his uniform looking intimidating.

"Reno, we're not actually going to do this, are we?" Kyle asked

"Yeah, I think we are," I said.

Ed got a big smile on his face. "Cool."

"Oh God, you guys *are* nuts," Kyle said. "If we end up in jail, I'm going to kill all of you."

Bird and I walked into the bar while Kyle and Ed waited outside. It took a minute or two, but we spotted Candy and her tall friend sitting at a table near the dance floor with their backs to us. We went back outside and made sure that Kyle and Ed were ready. They were, so we walked inside to carry out Bird's plan.

Kyle and Ed stood just inside the door, while Bird and I made our way toward Candy and her friend. As we walked, Bird danced and sang along to the song that was playing; "Come On Eileen" by Dexy's Midnight Runners.

I punched Bird on the arm, and pointed at the women, urging him to keep walking and to stop screwing around. He just shrugged. Thankfully, Candy and her friend still faced the dance floor, so they hadn't seen us approach.

"Hello, ladies," Bird said. The women sat at a small, round table. We moved to either side of them, Bird between them on one side of the table and me between them on the other.

"Oh God," Candy said.

"Who are these guys?" the tall girl asked Candy.

"These are the guys from this afternoon," Candy said. Her breathy voice suddenly didn't seem so sexy. The tall girl immediately reached for the purse that was sitting on the table, but I beat her to it.

"I'll hold this for you," I said.

"You know, ladies, what you did to us this afternoon was not very nice," Bird said. "But we don't want any trouble. We just want our money back."

When Bird mentioned the money, Candy looked down at the backpack sitting on the floor next to her chair. Bird grabbed the backpack, and held it away from Candy, who was trying to snag it from him.

"You may not want any trouble, but you're going to have plenty if we start screaming," the tall girl said.

"If you scream," Bird said, "that nice police officer over there by the door with our friend Kyle will be happy to come sort this out. You remember Kyle, don't you Candy? Should I call him and his new friend over?"

Both women went silent.

"Now, Candy, should I take your whole backpack or would you like to tell me where the money is?" Bird asked.

"It's in the front pocket in an envelope," Candy said.

"Candy!" the tall girl said.

"What do you want me to do? Do you want that cop over here?" Candy asked. The tall girl slumped in her chair, but said nothing.

Bird unzipped the front pocket of the backpack and removed the envelope. He handed the backpack to Candy. "It's a shame we couldn't have met under different circumstances," Bird said in a soft, sincere voice.

Candy rolled her eyes.

"Not now, Bird," I said. "Let's go."

Bird wasn't listening. "Candy, I feel like we should kiss. What do you think? Just one goodbye kiss?"

"Leave," Candy said, turning her back to Bird.

Bird acted like Candy's words had hurt him. He put his hands on his chest as if his heart was breaking. "All right, then," he said. He turned to the tall girl who was still sitting slumped in her chair. "It was nice meeting you."

The tall girl raised her right hand and gave him the finger.

"So much anger." Bird shook his head as we walked away.

Kyle and Ed stood at the door. "Did you get it?" Kyle asked.

"Yeah, let's go." I was anxious to get out of the bar.

When we got outside, Ed asked, "What now?"

"We should get out of here before they call the cops."

"Kyle, they're not going to call the cops," Bird said.

"Even so, it's probably not a good idea to hang around here," I said. I knew Bird was probably right, but I didn't see the sense in taking any chances.

"I'm starved," Ed said. "I know a great Mexican place on the other side of town, and you can pick up the tab to pay for my invaluable services."

Bird slapped Ed on the back and laughed. "Lugubrious," he said.

We got into our cars and headed out of the parking lot. As we drove away from the bar, Bird asked, "Hey guys, how much did Candy steal from us?"

"I think we figured out it was about four hundred and fifty bucks," I answered.

"Wow, it looks like Candy and her friend have been busy," Bird said. "There's over three thousand dollars in this envelope."

There was a brief moment of silence, and then Kyle blurted out, "Oh my God, we just robbed those women. We *are* going to jail."

"We didn't rob them," Bird said. "We just collected interest on the money we loaned them earlier today."

I laughed. "That's one way to think about it."

"What are we going to do now?" Kyle asked.

Nobody answered for several moments.

"Three thousand bucks," Bird whispered. "We can do just about anything we want."

I was about to say something when Bird asked, "Do you think there are any hookers in Rancho Cucamonga?"

§

Ed ordered a pitcher of margaritas for the table. "These guys are paying," he said to the waitress, "so keep them coming."

The restaurant was a hole in the wall that sat in a dingy strip shopping center. The walls were covered with black and white photos of old Mexico, along with a few obligatory velvet paintings of bullfights. Tinny music played from speakers in the ceiling. A woman with a mournful voice sang in Spanish, and two waitresses standing near the bar sang along.

Kyle shook his head and stared at Ed. "What the hell is going on with you?"

"What do you mean?" Ed asked.

"I thought you came out here to be a financial analyst," Kyle said. "Now you're some sort of private cop at a jewelry store? What happened?"

Ed let out a laugh. "Oh, that," he said. "I guess I should have warned you before you came out here and found out for yourself, but I didn't want word to get back to my old man. He still doesn't know that I quit my job."

"Your dad still thinks you're a financial analyst?"

Ed nodded. "Yeah, he does."

"Why did you quit," Kyle asked.

"The whole reason I came out to California in the first place was because I wanted to be a screenwriter. I've always wanted to write for the movies, but Dad wanted me to get a responsible job." Ed mocked his father's voice as he parroted the last few words, putting air quotes around them.

"You're a screenwriter?" Kyle asked, a sour look on his face.

"I haven't sold anything yet," Ed said, "but I'm working on a few spec scripts."

Kyle shook his head.

The waitress brought a pitcher of margaritas and four glasses to our table. She took our food orders, and Ed said something to her in Spanish. The waitress giggled.

"What did you say?" Kyle asked after the waitress had walked away.

"I told her the three of you are homos, and I'm the only straight one here."

Kyle wasn't amused. "You didn't really say that, did you?"

"I did." Ed took a long pull from his drink.

"Since when do you speak Spanish? I thought you took French in school."

"I did, but Spanish is more useful out here," Ed said.

"I want to make a toast," Bird said. "To our successful operation tonight, and the heroic role Ed played in it."

"To Ed," I said.

"To me," Ed said.

We all took generous slurps of our margaritas, except Kyle, who took a small sip and then put his glass down.

"I still can't believe you quit a perfectly good job to chase some pipe dream," Kyle said. "Couldn't you have kept the job, and just written at night?"

Ed had been laughing, but stopped when Kyle asked his question. "God, you sound like my dad. It's not a pipe dream, Kyle. It's what I want to do with my life." Ed took a drink from his margarita, and lowered his voice. "I tried writing at night, but I was always too tired after working a long day. I couldn't think clearly enough to write anything decent. Now I can write during the day, and do a brainless job at night."

"But all that money," Kyle said.

"There's more to life than money," Ed said.

Kyle was about to say something when the waitress came with our food.

"This looks great," Bird said to the waitress. She smiled, then walked away.

"Dig in, Boys," Ed said. "This is better than any Mexican food you've ever had back in Illinois."

"That waitress is good looking. Do you know her?" Bird asked Ed, stuffing a bite of burrito into his mouth.

"Not really. I just see her when I come in here to eat. But remember, she thinks you like guys."

"I love a challenge," Bird said.

Kyle was sullen. He remained quiet as we ate, and after dinner sat back in his chair with his arms crossed while the rest of us polished off another pitcher of margaritas.

"What do you guys have planned for San Francisco?" Ed asked.

I waited for Kyle to answer, but he remained quiet. "We're following in Jack Kerouac's footsteps," I said. "We want to find anything related to him."

"Kerouac?" Ed asked. "Have you ever read *The Dharma Bums*?"

"No, but I hear it's good."

"It's about how Kerouac got into Buddhism while he was up in Frisco. It's a great book. Really uplifting. I started going to American Buddhism meetings after reading it.

"Now you're a Buddhist?" Kyle almost shouted, breaking his silence.

"No, Kyle, I'm not a Buddhist. I'm not anything. I just wanted to see what it was all about."

Kyle sat back and crossed his arms again.

Ed drank the last remnants of his margarita. "Maybe we should get going. They'll be closing soon."

Bird and I finished our drinks and we all stood from the table.

"Thank you for coming in," the waitress said.

"Just to be clear," Bird said, leaning toward the waitress and talking low. "I'm not gay."

The waitress looked confused. "Oh, okay," she said.

Ed began laughing, and led the way out of the restaurant.

§

In San Francisco, we were supposed to stay with a friend of Bird's from high school—some guy named Brian—but on our way north along the coast, Bird admitted that he had never called Brian to make the arrangements.

"Where are we supposed to stay?" Kyle asked.

"I can call him now," Bird said. "I'm sure he won't mind if we crash at his place."

"Do you have his number?" I asked.

"No, but I'm sure I can get it."

"How are you going to get it?" Kyle asked.

"If it's not in the phone book, I can call some people who have it."

The Go-Go's were on the radio singing "We Got the Beat," but none of us sang along.

"If worst comes to worst, we can always get a hotel room. We still have plenty of Candy's money," Bird said.

"I told you I'm not going to use any of that money," Kyle said. After we had gotten the money from Candy, Kyle made it clear that all he wanted was the money that she had stolen from him, but didn't want to have anything to do with the rest.

"Why are you so uptight?" Bird asked.

"Because it's stolen money."

"You're such a fucking cub scout," Bird said.

Kyle looked at Bird in the rearview mirror and shook his head. I sympathized with Kyle, but only part-way. Candy had stolen from us, and it was just dumb luck that we had ended up with so much of her cash. We hadn't set out to rob her.

At Ed's suggestion, we drove up the coast on State Route 1. It would take longer, he told us, but he said the scenery was gorgeous. He was right. The central coast was beautiful, with beaches and rocky coastline to the west, and rugged mountain ranges to the east.

"I still can't believe that Ed quit a great job to become a screenwriter," Kyle said.

"It's what he wants to do, Kyle. What's wrong with pursuing his dream?" Bird asked.

"It's a silly dream. He already had a good job making great money."

"It's his dream, not yours." Bird raised his voice and leaned toward Kyle.

"Hey, let's drop this," I said. "We need to be more concerned with finding a place to stay tonight than with what Ed is doing with his life."

Bird sat back in his seat and let out a sigh. "Pull over here and I'll try to get Brian's number," he said.

We were in San Luis Obispo near the state university. Kyle parked, and we went in search of a payphone. Bird stopped a woman, and asked her if she knew where we could find one.

"There's one right over there in the university union," she said.

"Which one's that?" I asked.

"That's where I'm going. You can follow me."

"To the ends of the earth," Bird said.

She smiled. "This way." She walked and we fell in behind to her. "Where are you from?" she asked.

Her name was Megan, and we told her we were from Illinois. We explained that we needed to contact Bird's friend Brian so we'd have a place to stay in San Francisco.

"I live across the Bay in Hayward. In fact I'm heading home tomorrow for the summer. Where does your friend live?"

"I'm not sure," Bird said. "I just know he lives in or near San Francisco."

"You don't know where he lives and you don't know his telephone number. Are you sure you really know this guy?" Kyle asked.

"I know him," Bird said.

Megan laughed. She had a surfer girl look with thick blond hair swept back and slightly curled, a thin, fit body, and a big, bright smile.

Inside the university union, Megan showed us to the pay phone. We thanked her for helping us and she walked away. Bird picked up the receiver on the phone and began to dial, but then hung up and said to us, "I'll be right back." He went running off in the direction Megan had gone.

"God, why can't he keep his hormones in check?" Kyle asked.

"Can you blame him? She's gorgeous." Saying the words out loud made me wonder why I hadn't gone after Megan. I had gotten in the habit of waiting for Bird to act, and then following his lead.

A couple minutes later Bird came running back, out of breath.

"Did you catch her?" I asked.

Bird smiled and held up his hand. A phone number had been scrawled on his palm in blue ink.

"You got *her* phone number. Now can you get Brian's?" Kyle asked.

"Why do you have to be such a buzz kill?" Bird asked.

"I get this way when I don't have a place to stay."

I could tell that Bird wanted to respond, but he knew as well as we did that we were in this predicament because of him. He turned toward the telephone and started dialing.

Bird dialed information and found out that there was no listing for Brian. Next, he called his mom and got a phone number for his friend Kate. Kate didn't know Brian's number, but thought that Andy might know it. Andy wasn't home, but his brother said he worked with Brian's sister, Sara, and although he didn't have her number, his friend Heather had it. Heather gave Bird Sara's phone number. She wasn't home, but her boyfriend said Bird could call her at work. Bird called the number Sara's boyfriend gave him, asked for Sara, and then was put on hold. When Sara finally picked up, she gave Brian's number to Bird. Bird dialed Brian's number, but there was no answer. He left a message on the answering machine. The whole ordeal took almost two hours, and several dollars' worth of quarters.

We got back into the car and headed north again, hoping that Brian would get home before we made it to San Francisco. We continued on State Route 1 heading up the coast and stopped in Carmel to try Brian again. Bird left another message. He tried yet again when we got to Santa Cruz and this time he hit the jackpot. Brian was home.

According to Bird, Brian was happy to hear from him and he invited us to stay at his apartment. He lived close to downtown San Francisco and was a musician. Bird wasn't sure what instrument Brian played—maybe a trumpet or a trombone, he said—or what type of music he performed. In fact, there was a lot Bird didn't know about him. Like Kyle, I was beginning to wonder just how well Bird knew Brian.

We followed the directions Brian had provided, and ended up in front of a Vietnamese restaurant in San Francisco's Tenderloin District. Brian had an apartment above the restaurant.

"There's something I want to tell you guys before you meet Brian," Bird said, as we were getting out of the car. "He's gay."

"You didn't think to tell us that before?" Kyle said.

"What's the big deal?" I asked. "We're just crashing at his place, not dating him."

"I could set you up with him if you're interested," Bird said.

"No thanks, but what if he comes on to me?" Kyle asked.

"Why would he come on to you? You're not gay, are you?"

"No, of course not. But for some reason, gay guys like me."

Bird and I laughed. "What do you mean gay guys like you?" I asked.

"There's a gay guy at my dad's bank and he's always looking at me when I'm there."

"That's your proof? Some guy you think is gay looks at you?"

"He is gay. He brought his boyfriend or partner or whatever they call them to the bank Christmas party."

"And you think he's attracted to you because he looks at you?"

"Yes."

"If Brian was going to come on to one of us, why would he choose you over Reno or me? What makes you think you're a gay guy's fantasy?"

"I don't know, Kyle said, lowering his voice. "They just seem to like me."

"Bird, over here," a voice called from a doorway next to the restaurant.

We were standing behind Kyle's car hauling our luggage from the trunk. Bird waved at Brian.

"When I introduce you to Brian, try not to be so irresistible, Kyle. Give the poor guy a fighting chance."

"Very funny," Kyle said. He shut the trunk and walked behind Bird and me as we approached Brian's door.

Brian's apartment was a small studio that consisted of a large room that served as the kitchen, living room, and bedroom, and a separate, very small bathroom. It was neat and clean, but it was only about half the size of Ed's apartment in Rancho Cucamonga.

"Bird, I still can't believe you called. I was so surprised. I wish you would have called sooner. I could have gone shopping."

"We kind of wish he'd called sooner, too." Kyle said.

"I shouldn't be surprised," Brian said. "Bird has always been crazy and impulsive like this. It's good to see you haven't changed."

"It would be nice if he changed a little," Kyle said.

Bird gave Kyle a hard look. "You have a roof over your head. Why can't you stop bitching?"

"After all the shit you've pulled this trip, you're worried about a little complaining?"

"Ladies, let's not fight," Brian said. "This apartment is too small for hard feelings. Let's all get along."

"Good idea," I said. "I'm exhausted, but I could go for a drink. Do you have any beer?

"No beer, but I have some wine." Brian went into the kitchen and pulled a bottle of wine off of a rack on the counter that held five or six bottles. He held up one of the bottles. "A little red to celebrate your visit?"

We gathered around the kitchen counter and Brian poured a glass for each of us. We took our wine into the living room and sat down. "To San Francisco," I said.

Everyone raised their glasses in a toast.

"Did Bird ever tell you about the time we slept together?" Brian asked. I almost spit out my wine.

"He never mentioned it," Kyle said. "Why don't you tell us?"

I looked at Bird, expecting him to protest, but he sat quietly with a silly grin on his face.

"It was our senior year in high school," Brian began. "He and I were in bed together and there were about two or three hundred people watching us."

"What?" Kyle blurted out.

"Just tell them the story," Bird said. He was calm, sitting back on the couch sipping his wine.

Brian laughed. "Okay, I'll stop teasing. Bird and I played Oscar and Felix in *The Odd Couple*. You could probably guess that he was Oscar and I was Felix. In one of the scenes, we were in bed together. That became the joke during our senior year; that Bird and I had slept together."

"I'm slightly disappointed," I said.

"So was I," Brian said. We all laughed. "But it was during that play that I decided what I wanted to do with my life. I knew I wanted to be on stage, acting and playing music. I've been lucky enough to do that for the past few years."

"Bird told us that you're a musician, but I didn't know you acted, too. Are you in any plays now?" I asked.

"Not right now. I play keyboards in a band and I pick up a little work as a studio musician. That pays the bills. I have an audition next week for a production of *Waiting for Godot*."

"It's great that you figured out what you want to do with your life," I said. "I wish I could."

"What do you mean?" Bird asked. "I thought you wanted to be a writer."

"I'd love to be a writer, but almost nobody can make a living just from writing. They all have other jobs. I need to find a way to make some money before I worry about writing, and even then, my dad eventually wants me to help him build his business. I'm not sure if I'll ever have time to write."

Maybe you'll just have to defy your dad like Ed did. After all, it's your life," Bird said.

Kyle snorted. "Ed was stupid to give up the security of a good job to chase an iffy dream that doesn't pay anything. Reno. You don't want to do that."

"Who's Ed?" Brian asked.

We explained who Ed was, and about his decision to quit his job to become a screenwriter.

Brian sipped his wine. "It's risky, but I wouldn't say it's stupid, not if it's what he really wants to do."

"That's what I said," Bird said.

Kyle had a disgusted look on his face, and shook his head.

"What is it that you want to do with your life, Bird?" Brian asked.

"I just want to be happy in whatever I do. I'd rather be poor and happy than rich and miserable. I'll figure out some way to make money."

"Sounds nice, but I don't think that's how it works," Kyle said. "Nobody's going to pay you to be happy. They pay you to work."

"So why can't you do work that makes you happy?" Bird asked.

"Everyone wants to be happy in their work, but there are damn few jobs out there that are fun. A handful of people get those jobs and everyone else works for a living. Not everyone can be happy in their work. That's just how it is."

"You might be right," I said. "When I look at my parents, they like their jobs okay, but I don't think they're really happy. They have a lot of responsibility and they have to do a lot of shit they'd rather not do. It's the same thing with their friends. Some of them even make really good money, but I don't think any of them are truly happy."

"That's what I mean," Kyle said. "Having a job is about making money and paying the bills. If you want to be happy, go golfing on the weekend or take up some other hobby. Jobs don't make you happy."

"I'm happy with my job," Brian said. "It's exactly what I want to do."

"No offense," Kyle said, "but look at the lifestyle your job provides." Kyle looked around the small room. "This apartment might be good enough for now, but how are you going to feel in five or ten years when your friends have moved on and they're making more money and buying bigger houses and driving nicer, more expensive cars. You'll be left behind and then your job won't seem so great."

"But why do you have to buy bigger houses and nicer cars? Just because your friends do?" Bird asked. "That's a sucky reason. Instead, why can't you scale back what you want and be happy with what you have?"

"Because it doesn't happen," Kyle said. "I mean, it sounds good in theory, but for most people, they see their friends doing better in life, and suddenly the small apartment and the low paying job that used to make them happy no longer does. There's a reason people get an education, start a career, get married, buy a house, have kids, and on and on. It's because it's a proven script. Trying to live a different kind of life is a romantic notion, but long-term, it doesn't work."

"Reno, do you agree with this shit?" Bird asked.

"I like the idea of living a different kind of life where your work and your home life both make you happy, but I've never seen anyone do it. I wish it was possible, but there must be a reason people follow Kyle's script," I said.

"That's just depressing," Bird said. "What about the way that Kerouac and his buddies lived, traveling around and enjoying themselves? They seemed happy."

"Happy?" Kyle asked. "They were drug addicts and alcoholics who lived in squalor most of their lives. Kerouac drank himself to death. Neal Cassady passed out from doing drugs down in Mexico, and died from exposure. They had fun in short bursts, but overall, they were poor and miserable."

"That's depressing," I said.

"I practically want to kill myself. There's no use going on." Bird put his hands around his throat and acted like he was choking himself.

"You know what they say," Brian said. "Life's a bitch and then you die."

"Very uplifting. Thanks for the positive words. Is there any more wine?" Bird asked.

Brian retreated to the kitchen and fetched another bottle. "Why the interest in Kerouac?" he asked.

We told him about the class we had taken where we read *On the Road*, and how our trip was a kind of re-creation of Sal Paradise's journey in the novel.

"You know, Kerouac spent a lot of time around San Francisco," Brian said. "Some of those guys Kerouac hung out with were gay or they openly experimented with homosexuality."

"How do you know that?" Kyle asked.

"It's just common knowledge around here. Kerouac talked a little bit about gays in the book—he mostly called us queers—and because of it, there was talk of banning the book. A lot of those beats would sleep with anyone and everyone."

"Where did he hang out around here?" I asked.

"In the book, he talked a lot about Mill City," Kyle said.

"I don't know of anywhere around here called Mill City," Brian said. "There's a bookstore on Columbus Avenue that always has Kerouac stuff in their windows. You could probably find out more from them."

We went to City Lights Bookstore the next day. When we told the woman at the front desk that we wanted to find out about Jack Kerouac's exploits in San Francisco, she introduced us to a tall, skinny guy named Martin Hale. Martin looked to be in his thirties or forties, with long, stringy hair, and a shaggy beard. He talked like he was perpetually high.

"Yeah man, Kerouac used to come to the bookstore with Neal Cassady and Allen Ginsburg. They were friends with the owner, Lawrence Ferlinghetti. Have you read Kerouac's books?"

"We read *On the Road*," I said.

"Yeah, that's cool. You should read *Dharma Bums*. That's his best one."

"So we've heard. Do you know much about where he hung out while he was in San Francisco?" I asked.

"Are you guys, like, on a vision quest or something? Far out. Kerouac lived with Neal Cassady in a little house on Russell Street over in Nob Hill. I'm not sure of the address. They used to hang out and drink at Vesuvio Café."

"Where's that?" Kyle asked.

Martin motioned for us to follow him and he walked to the front corner of the store, pointing at a side window. Across a small alleyway sat Vesuvio Café. "You won't even have to move your car, man."

"Cool," Bird said. "We heard that there's no place in San Francisco called Mill City, like in the book. Do you have any idea where Kerouac was talking about?"

"Yeah, he was talking about up in Marin County, just over the bridge. He combined the name Marin City and Mill Valley to come up with Mill City. You know the part in the book where Sal is staying with Remi Boncoeur and Remi gets him a job as a night watchman? That's in Mill Valley."

We thanked Martin and made plans to meet up with him later that day at Vesuvio to talk more about Kerouac. When we left, we followed Martin's directions to Russell Street, but we had no idea which house had once belonged to Neal Cassady. The houses were small, clapboard-sided structures that were built close together, one right next to the other. A couple of the houses had been fixed up with fresh paint, but most were weather-worn and tired looking. We stopped a couple of people on the street to ask if they knew where Neal Cassady had once lived or where Jack Kerouac stayed, but they didn't know what we were talking about. We gave up and headed to Mill Valley.

We were disappointed that we weren't getting the Jack Kerouac experience we had expected when we started our trip. Actually, I'm not sure what we expected. Whatever it was, our expectations weren't being met.

We crossed the Golden Gate Bridge and drove another twenty minutes north to Mill Valley. We didn't know what we were looking for, and I could tell that Kyle was getting annoyed. He wasn't real excited about our trip to begin with. Now that we were wandering around aimlessly, he was not a happy camper.

"Do we even know what we're looking for?" Kyle asked.

"Can't you just enjoy looking around? It's not like we have other plans," Bird said.

Kyle looked straight ahead as he drove. "If we're not going to actually do something, I'd just as soon go home. Smilin' Sam was right. Kerouac sucked, and this trip to follow in his footsteps is starting to suck, too."

I had gotten the feeling earlier that Kyle didn't want to continue our trip once he saw Ed. Seeing his friend had been an excuse to put up with Bird through Denver and Las Vegas. Now, the excuse was gone.

"Maybe we could check in at the library to see if they know anything about Kerouac there." I said. "It beats just driving around."

We found the library, and we all went in to see what we could learn. It wasn't much. The librarian, an older woman with gray hair and a purple flower print dress, said that Kerouac used to live with a poet by the name of Gary Snyder.

"Do you know where they lived?" Bird asked.

"They lived in a cabin at 370 Montford," she said, without having to look up the information.

"We should go there," I said.

"I can give you directions," the librarian said, "but I'm afraid the cabin isn't there anymore. It was torn down several years ago."

"Oh, great," Kyle said. "Another dead end."

"They did build another house on the land where the cabin used to be, but it's not the same place Kerouac stayed, I'm afraid. If you want to know more about Kerouac's time at the cabin, you should read *The Dharma Bums*. He writes about his experiences here in Mill Valley in that book. It's one of my favorites. I think it's better than *On the Road*."

We thanked the librarian for her time and headed back to the car.

"So what are we going to do now?" Kyle asked.

"Let's go by where the cabin used to be," Bird said.

"Why? It isn't there anymore."

"We don't have anything else to do," I said. "We might as well drive by before we head back to San Francisco."

We ended up on a narrow road in a rundown part of town. On one side of the road, the land sloped down into a valley. On the other—the side where Kerouac's cabin had once stood—the land went up a hill. The area was heavily treed, and where the cabin had been, there was now a small house. In the front yard were several long logs, and an assortment of axes and handsaws.

"We drove all the way to California to see this? I could have driven around Chicago and seen slums," Kyle said.

"First of all, this isn't a slum," Bird said. "Not everyone can live in a mansion. And second, this is all part of the adventure. It's part of the experience."

"Driving past houses where Kerouac never lived is an adventure? This sucks."

"Why do you always—"

"Maybe we should just head back and get something to eat," I said. "I'm hungry." I looked back at Bird and hoped my look conveyed my desire for us not to fight. He must have gotten the message.

"Yeah, I'm hungry too. Let's go eat."

Kyle turned on the radio and we heard Blondie sing "Call Me." After that, "Billie Jean" by Michael Jackson came on. The three of us were quiet.

We stopped at a fast food joint, and after we had eaten, Kyle said he needed to call Joan. He went to use the pay phone, and Bird and I stayed at the table.

"What the hell is his deal?" Bird asked. "All he does is bitch."

"I guess he's frustrated we aren't seeing more Kerouac stuff," I said.

"Did he think we were going to see Kerouac and hang out with him?"

"He's getting pressure from Joan to go home. I know he feels like he let his dad down by taking this trip instead of working at the bank."

"I just wish he'd try to enjoy the ride rather than ruining it for us," Bird said.

After lunch, we headed to Vesuvio Café for drinks. Martin said he would be stopping by after work.

We got a table and each ordered a Coors. The bar was full of what my dad would call "characters." There was a guy sitting at the bar wearing a tank top and a tie-dyed cowboy hat. Next to him was a guy with dreadlocks wearing a long overcoat and sunglasses. A guy dressed like the captain on "The Love Boat" walked into the bar, looked around, and then walked out. Nobody paid attention to any of these people. The weirdness was apparently expected.

There was still tension between Bird and Kyle. Each drank his beer and didn't talk. I wanted to talk, but couldn't think of anything to say. So we all sat quietly drinking and looking around the bar.

"Did you guys just come from a funeral?" the waitress asked.

Bird laughed. What's your name?" he asked.

"Brandy, but you can call me Brandy."

"What do I get if I order Brandy?" Bird asked.

"More than you can handle," she said.

"In that case, I'll have a double."

"Good come-back," she said. "Are you guys ready for another round?"

"We'd be foolish not to," Bird said.

When Brandy walked to the bar to get our drinks, Kyle said, "She's good looking."

"Yes she is, man," Martin said, walking up to the table. "Looks like you got a head start on me."

Brandy brought our drinks and gave Martin a hug once she had set the bottles on our table. "What do you want, Sweetie?" she asked Martin.

"I think I'll start with a bourbon. I've got some catching up to do." Brandy walked away and Martin sat down at our table. "Did you find Neal Cassady's house?"

"We drove down Russell Street, but nobody seemed to know which house was his," Bird said. "The street's only a block long. We must have seen it. We just didn't know which one it was."

Kyle let out a sarcastic laugh and took a pull from his beer.

"Oh man, I've never gone over there, even though it's just a few minutes away. I should go sometime and figure it out," Martin said.

Brandy brought Martin's drink, winked at him, and walked away.

"We went over to Mill Valley too, but we didn't see anything there either," Kyle said. "It was a real red letter day."

Bird sat back in his chair and glared at Kyle, who didn't seem to notice.

"We saw where Kerouac's cabin used to be," I said, "but it was torn down a long time ago. There's another house there now."

Martin raised his glass and drank down about two-thirds of the bourbon. When he stopped drinking, he let out a sigh. "Man, that first drink of the day is so good."

"After that drink, I think you might have caught up to us already," Bird said.

Martin laughed, then leaned over the table like he was going to tell us a secret. He motioned for us to lean, too. "Do you guys smoke?" he asked, raising the pinched thumb and pointer finger of his right hand to his lips.

"No," Kyle said at exactly the same time as Bird said, "Yes,"

Martin looked back and forth between Kyle and Bird, then shook his head in confusion.

"We have, but not much," I said, trying to explain. "We mostly just drink."

"I got you, man. I'm going to the alley to toke up. If you're interested in joining me, come on."

Martin stood from the table, and Bird immediately stood. I was the next to get up, which left Kyle the only one still sitting.

"What the hell," Kyle said, and he stood up, too.

"All right then, it's unanimous."

"You're not leaving already, are you?" Brandy asked.

"Save our seats, Darlin'. We'll be right back," Martin said.

We walked outside into the alley that ran between the café and the bookstore. "Welcome to Adler Alley," Martin said. He took a baggie out of his pocket and removed a joint. "This isn't your normal pot, man. This is strong stuff, so be warned."

"But it's just pot, right?" Kyle asked.

"It is, but it's not your granddaddy's weak Illinois weed. This is some A-number-one, primo shit."

Martin lit the joint and handed it to Bird. He took a long drag and held it in as he passed the joint to me. I put it to my lips and inhaled. I tried to hold the smoke in, but started coughing. I took another hit and passed the joint to Kyle. He looked around at us, but just held the joint in his hand.

"Take a hit, man," Martin said. "Don't let it burn down."

Kyle raised the joint to his mouth and took a quick drag. He seemed surprised that he hadn't coughed. So he took a bigger drag and held it in.

"That's it," Martin said as he took the joint back from Kyle.

We passed the joint around, and with each rotation, Kyle became bolder and took ever bigger, deeper hits.

"Is the first joint of the day as good as the first drink?" I asked Martin.

"It is," he said, "but this isn't the first joint of the day."

We polished off two joints before we went back into the bar. On the way in, Martin put his arm around Kyle's shoulder, and said, "I'm proud of you, man. You're like the illegitimate son I never had." Kyle smiled dumbly.

Martin was right. The marijuana was strong stuff. I felt peaceful and everything around me seemed to be swirling and running down a bright drain. Bird was smiling and looking around the bar. He hadn't spoken in several minutes.

Kyle's eyes were slits, and he had a dreamy look on his face. He kept saying, "That was some good shit."

"Look who's back," Brandy said. "Did you save any for me?"

"There's always some for you," Martin said.

We sat back at the table where our drinks were waiting for us.

"Brandy, did you know that we have three young Kerouac scholars in our midst tonight?" Martin said, pointing at us. "They're beatniks in training."

"Is that right?"

"I think they each need a Jack Kerouac to quench their thirst for knowledge," Martin said. The second half of the sentence he spoke with an exaggerated, elitist accent. Despite his best efforts, he couldn't keep his normal hippie burnout voice from coming through. "And one for me."

Brandy nodded, and walked toward the bar.

"What's a Jack Kerouac?" I asked.

"It's the house specialty," he said.

"A Jerk Kerouac," Kyle said and laughed at his verbal stumble. We all laughed at Kyle laughing at himself.

Brandy brought four drinks and set one down in front of each of us. "A Jack Kerouac for each and every one of you," she said.

"Jerk Kerouac," Kyle said and started laughing again.

"What's in this?" I asked.

"Taste it first and tell me if you like it," Brandy said.

I tilted the glass back and took a drink. "It's good," I said.

"It has rum and tequila mixed with orange juice, cranberry juice, and lime juice."

"It's delicious," Kyle said, although he hadn't tried any of his drink.

"These will go on my tab," Martin said. "It's my gift to the youth of America."

"Yeah," Bird said, slapping Martin on the back. "He's a real gone cat. He knows time."

"Yeah man, now you're talking like a beatnik. These Jack Kerouacs really do work."

"Jerk Kerouac," Kyle said again.

"Lugubrious."

§

When we got back to Brian's apartment he was gone. There was a note on the table that read,

If you make it home alive, come to Aunt Charlie's (133 Turk Street).

We had no idea what Aunt Charlie's was or where Turk Street was, but we were game for just about anything. Thankfully, Brian had included directions.

Aunt Charlie's was a few blocks from Brian's apartment. We probably could have walked. We probably should have walked considering how drunk and high we were, but we didn't. We found a parking spot down the street and walked to the bar.

The building was nothing special. The front was green and needed paint. There was a neon sign in the front window and another one over the door that read "Aunt Charlie's Lounge." When we walked in, we were assailed by bright pink neon lights that cut through the din of smoke. The smell of burning tobacco and an odd combination of perfume and body odor permeated the air. Unless I was seeing double or triple, there were multiple women walking around the bar looking a lot like Marilyn Monroe. It felt like we had walked into the middle of a carnival.

"Bird," I heard a voice call. Brian was sitting with two other guys at a table near the door.

"Where have you all been?" Brian asked.

"We were at a place called Vesuvio Café," Bird said.

"Best place in the world," Kyle said, slowly. He introduced himself to Brian's friends. "Hi, I'm Kyle."

Bird and I followed suit. Brian's friends were Hector, a balding Hispanic man in an expensive suit, and Michael, a black guy with an impressive build and a velour pull over top.

"Looks like somebody had a good time at Vesuvio," Brian said, nodding at Kyle. Kyle was oblivious.

"It's a fun place," Bird said.

"It's the beatnik headquarters of Frisco," Michael said.

"That's why we were there," I said. "We're following the Kerouac trail."

"Jack Kerouac was a misogynist and a queen," Hector said with his thick Spanish-by-way-of-New-York accent.

"What do you mean?" Bird asked. "Kerouac was married and had kids."

"That's true, but that doesn't prevent a man from being gay. Just ask Michael."

"It's true," Michael said. "I was married for almost five years."

"You're gay?" Kyle asked.

"I am," Michael said. "And Hector's my partner, so don't get any ideas."

Everyone laughed except Kyle, who took a step away from Hector. "But you're so big."

"What's that mean?" Michael asked. "You think only little guys can be gay?"

"No, but…So you're all gay?" Kyle asked, pointing at Brian, Hector and Michael.

"Honey, with the exception of you Kerouac freaks, everyone in this place is gay," Hector said.

"This is a gay bar?" Kyle asked.

"Yes." Brian laughed. "Is that a problem?"

"I've just never been in a gay bar before. I'm not sure how to act."

"Maybe you should order a drink," Bird said.

"Waitress," Brian called to a short blond with pig tails two tables over. She turned around and we saw a man with a thick black mustache.

"What can I get for you, honey?" she asked in a low voice.

Kyle couldn't speak. He opened his mouth, but no words came out.

"Do you have Coors?" I asked.

The waitress said that they did, and I ordered a round.

Kyle was still staring at the thick mustachioed waitress when she walked away.

"I can get you her number if you're interested," Hector said.

"No, that's okay," Kyle said.

The waitress with the mustache brought our beers. "If you need anything else, just let me know," she said, then winked at Kyle.

"I think she likes you," Michael said.

Everyone laughed except Kyle.

"Before you guys got here, we were talking over a problem," Brian said. "Michael is supposed to sing at a big open mic night here tomorrow night, but his background singers can't make it."

"More like they abandoned me," Michael said.

"Los pendejos," Hector said, and put his hand on Michael's arm.

"What are you going to do?" I asked.

"I'm going to have to cancel unless I can find more backup singers."

"You sing, Brian. Why don't you back him up?" Bird asked.

"I would, but our band is the house band here at Aunt Charlie's, and we're not allowed to compete in the open mic."

"Plus, we'd still need two more. We need three backup singers," Michael said. "I don't know what I'm going to do."

"We could do it," Kyle said. "There are three of us."

"You're drunk," Bird said. "Don't listen to him. He's drunk."

"And high," Kyle said.

"If I remember right," Brian said, "you used to be a pretty good singer, Bird. You should do this."

"Oh please, would you be willing to help?" Michael asked. He was smiling and suddenly looked hopeful.

"Reno, what do you think?" Bird asked.

"You're the one who's always talking about making your life an adventure. Here's your chance to practice what you preach," I said.

Bird took a long pull from his Coors. "Damn me and my adventure-seeking ways. You're right. I am always talking about that. I suppose this will be a great memory someday. We're in."

Michael quickly stood and hugged Bird. "Thank you so much. You saved the act."

§

The next afternoon we were in the basement of a community center getting ready to practice for our big night.

"Guys, I really don't want to do this," Kyle said.

"Too bad. You said we'd do it, so now we have to," Bird said.

"I was messed up. I didn't know what I was saying."

"It'll be fine," I added. "What are we supposed to be singing?"

"I don't know," Bird said. "Hopefully Michael will be here soon."

Just then Brian, Michael, and Hector walked in. Michael carried a boom box, and Brian and Hector carried suit bags.

"Sorry we're late," Brian said. "We had to pick up your tuxedos."

"Tuxedos?" I asked.

Brian laid the suit bags on a table and took one out. The tuxedo jacket was powder blue and it had matching pants with a dark blue strip down the side of the leg.

"We're wearing that?" Kyle asked.

"Not just that," Brian said. He opened another suit bag and pulled out a pink shirt with ruffles down the front. "You're going to wear this with a dark blue bow tie. You'll look fantastic."

"I don't want to wear that," Kyle said.

"But you promised," Michael said.

"Listen to me, hijo de puta," Hector said, "we rented these tuxedos and shirts because you said you would help Michael. You can't back out now." Hector took an angry step toward Kyle.

"Don't worry, we're going to do this, aren't we Kyle?" Bird said, putting his hand on Kyle's shoulder.

Kyle looked at Bird and then at Hector. "Yeah, we'll do it."

"Good," said Michael. "Now we have to practice."

Hector turned away from Kyle without speaking.

"What are we singing, anyway?" I asked.

"Midnight Train to Georgia," Michael said. "You're the Pips."

"Hey, we know that song," Bird said.

"And Hector's going to show you the dance moves."

Hector had moved across the room and was facing us. "Come over here and I'll show you where to stand."

We went over by Hector and he arranged us the way he wanted us to stand: Kyle and me on the sides and Bird in the middle. He then showed us three different moves which he called "the train," "the swing," and "the whistle."

"These are the only moves you need to know," Hector said. "Everything is based on these three moves."

We practiced the dance moves over and over again to a recording of Gladys Knight and the Pips that Hector played on the boom box. Michael and Brian stood across the room and interjected a thought now and then, but it was clear that Hector was in charge.

Just when I thought we were doing pretty well, Hector would yell, "Que diablos es eso?" and we'd start again from the beginning. We listened to the song over and over until our moves were second nature. Finally, he said, "I think you've got it."

"Can we quit now?" Kyle asked. "My feet hurt."

Brian stood with his hand on his chin. "I think that's as good as they're going to get."

"I hope it's good enough," Hector said.

Michael put his arm around Hector's waist. "We have to get going before the dry cleaner closes."

Hector told us we should be at Aunt Charlie's by 8:30, then he, Michael, and Brian left.

"I don't think I can do this," Kyle said. "It's one thing to do it here, but it's another to be in front of a crowd."

"You're not getting stage fright, are you?" Bird asked.

"I don't like being up in front of people. I thought I was going to get sick just giving a two minute presentation in speech class."

"You'll be fine," I said. "We all will."

We were walking to the car when Kyle suddenly stopped. "Guys, I'm serious. I don't think I can get up in front of a bunch of people and dance."

"You have to," I said. "Michael's counting on you."

"But I can't. I'm too nervous."

"I think I know what to do about that," Bird said. "Let's go to Vesuvio."

§

Martin was sitting by himself at the same table we had shared with him a day earlier. "Hey man, it's the Kerouacians. I've got a head start on you this time," he said, holding up his drink.

"Welcome back," Brandy said. "What are we drinking tonight?"

"How about a round of Coors?" Bird asked.

Brandy nodded and went to get our drinks.

"Did you make any big Jack Kerouac discoveries today?" Martin asked.

"Not today," Bird said. "We were busy practicing for our big debut."

"Debut? What are you talking about, man?"

We told Martin about the open mic contest at Aunt Charlie's and about our role as Pips backing up Michael's Gladys Knight.

"Aunt Charlie's is a gay bar, man. I didn't know you guys were gay."

"We're not gay," Kyle said, too loudly.

"I'll keep that in mind," Brandy said. She set our beers on the table.

"We're just helping out a gay friend," I said. "Actually, a friend of a friend."

"Who's gay, the friend or the friend of your friend?" Brandy asked.

"They both are," I said.

"Both are gay or both are friends," she asked.

"Yes," Bird said.

"Stop, man," Martin said. "You're hurting my head."

It was late afternoon, and the place was starting to fill up. The guy with the tie-dyed cowboy hat was back at the bar drinking some kind of colorful drink. Outside, a truck drove by and blasted its low, piercing horn.

"What are you guys even talking about?" Brandy asked.

We explained the whole thing again for Brandy's benefit.

"That is so cool that you guys are helping out a friend like that," she said. She spoke to all of us, but was looking directly at Bird.

"He's really more a friend of a friend," Bird said.

"Don't start again, man," Martin said. "Brandy, we should go see them tonight."

"I don't get off until eight," she said.

"The contest doesn't start until nine," Bird said. "Can you come after you get off work?"

"Yeah, I think so." Brandy was looking at Bird again, pausing for a beat too long before she turned to Martin and asked, "Do you want to drive?"

"Yeah, cool."

Brandy nodded to Martin, smiled again at Bird, and then walked away.

"I think she likes you, man," Martin said to Bird.

"Can you blame her?" Bird asked. We all laughed. "Martin, we have a favor to ask."

"Oh, oh," Martin said. "What do you need?"

Bird leaned across the table so he could talk quietly to Martin. "It's nothing bad. We just want to buy a couple of joints off you for tonight. It will help us relax."

"Mostly, it will help me relax," Kyle said. "I'm scared to death."

Martin nodded and smiled. "Yeah, man. I can do that. How much do you want?"

"Just a couple," Bird said.

"Better make it three," Kyle said.

"Look at you, man," Martin said. "Yesterday you didn't even know how to smoke, and today you're a head."

Everybody laughed except Kyle. "I'm not a head. I'm just nervous."

"Those things aren't mutually exclusive, man."

§

Bird and I sat in the tiny living room at Brian's waiting for Kyle to get done in the shower. Queen's "Fat Bottomed Girls" was playing on the stereo.

"Do you think Kyle is going to be okay?" I asked.

"Yeah, he'll be fine," Bird said. "If he ever wants to enjoy life, he's going to have to loosen up."

"I feel sorry for him. I know I didn't expect to come on this road trip and end up being a backup singer for a cross-dresser. He's probably kind of in shock"

Bird laughed. "I didn't expect it either, but it will be a fun experience. Not many people get to do this."

"I don't think many people want to do this."

"That's probably true, but most people are assholes who are afraid of trying something new and different. That's why most people never do anything with their lives."

"You think we have to be backup singers at a gay club to do something with our lives?"

Bird tilted back the beer he was drinking and finished it. "No, that's not what I'm saying. What we're doing isn't what's important. It's our willingness to do it."

I took Bird's empty and went into the kitchen to get us fresh beers. "You mean, because we're willing to be backup singers in a gay bar, we're going to have successful lives?"

"Something like that," he said, taking the fresh beer I had retrieved for him. "It's not a guarantee, but I think it sets you up to be more successful in life if you're willing to take chances and try new things."

I was actually a little surprised that Bird had thought about this kind of thing. I thought I was the only one among us who really pondered life. "It's scary, but I think I understand what you're saying. When did you become such a philosopher?" I asked.

He smiled. "I'm not just a pretty face."

When Kyle was done in the shower I took my turn. Maybe Bird was right. I never wanted to be like Kyle, afraid of trying new things and taking risks. I wanted to live a more adventurous life, full of new experiences. I had no idea how I could do it, but I wanted to avoid the scripted life of cubicles, expense accounts, and two weeks of vacation. I especially wanted to avoid working for my dad. If being a background singer at a gay bar could help me get there, I was all in.

When I got out of the shower, I put on the pink ruffled shirt and the light blue tuxedo. I looked ridiculous, but I kind of liked it. Kyle was complaining because his pants were too short.

"Look, the bottoms of my pants don't even touch my shoes."

"They don't look bad," I said. It was a lie.

"Maybe this will help," Bird said, lighting one of the joints Martin had sold us. Bird handed it to Kyle. He took a deep drag and held it in like a pro.

"I think you *are* becoming a head," I said to Kyle.

Kyle shook his head and after a moment released the smoke. "No I'm not," he said. "I'm just nervous."

"We need to get going," Bird said. "We're supposed to meet Gladys Knight and her entourage in fifteen minutes."

"Let's finish this first,' Kyle said, snagging the joint from my hand.

"No, you're definitely not turning into a head," I said.

§

At Aunt Charlie's, Kyle had trouble parking the car. He tried to back into a spot, but it took him four tries.

"I think I'm high," he said. "Maybe we should smoke another joint now."

We did.

When we went inside the bar, Brian and Hector were waiting for us. As usual, Hector was not happy.

"Where have you been? You were supposed to be here almost twenty minutes ago."

"We had trouble parking," Bird said.

"We really did," Kyle added.

"Where's Michael?" I asked.

"Here he comes now," Brian said.

Michael walked up to the table in a flowing dress a shade of pink darker than our shirts. He wore a thick, dark wig that fell to his shoulders, and had on a wide gold necklace. His eye shadow matched our shirts, and his lipstick was bright red.

"How do I look?" Michael asked.

"You look beautiful, mi amore," Hector said.

"You're gorgeous," Brian said.

"Is that Michael?" Kyle asked.

Martin and Brandy walked in, and I waved them over to our table.

"You guys look great," Brandy said. She looked different than she had at Vesuvio's: a little older and more dressed up. Her straight hair had been curled and she wore a short skirt that was both sexy and formal.

Based on the smitten look on Bird's face, it was obvious that he also noticed the difference. He gave Brandy a hug. "You look great, too," he said. "Let me get you and Martin a drink."

"I won't argue with that, man," Martin said.

Bird took Martin's drink order, then he and Brandy went to the bar.

"How's Kyle doing?" Martin asked me. Kyle stood on the other side of the table, still staring at Michael.

"He's kind of high, but I think he's going to be okay."

"You know," Martin said, "I feel bad about charging you for those joints earlier today, so I got you a present." Martin pulled a book from the bag he was carrying. "It's a biography of Jack Kerouac."

Martin handed me a hardcover book with a black-and-white photo of Kerouac on the cover. "Thanks, Martin. That was nice of you," I said.

"I read it, and really dug it," he said.

Bird and Brandy came back to the table and Bird handed Martin a rum and Coke. "Here's to a great night," Bird said. He raised his beer in a toast. Everyone at the table toasted and took a drink.

We stood around talking for another ten minutes when the lights dimmed and a man dressed like Marilyn Monroe stepped to the microphone.

"Hello everyone and welcome to Aunt Charlie's annual open mic competition," she said in a sultry voice. When she had welcomed everyone, she introduced the first act, a guy who sang "The Way of Love." She looked just like Cher, with long, dark hair, full lips, and dangly silver earrings. She sounded great.

The second act was another Marilyn Monroe impersonator singing Bonnie Tyler's "Total Eclipse of the Heart." There was a disconnect between the way the singer was dressed and the song. You could feel that the audience wasn't getting it.

"That's Tim Boylan," Michael said. "He always dresses like Marilyn, and he never wins."

"It's time for you to go backstage," Hector said. He led Michael through the crowd like he was escorting a bride down the aisle. We followed. Brandy gave Bird a kiss on the cheek and wished him good luck.

The third act was another guy dressed like Cher, but this time she was with a Sonny look-a-like. They sang "I Got You Babe." Both singers looked good, but they had trouble staying on key. At one point, Sonny seemed to forget the words.

When Sonny and Cher had finished, the MC introduced us as Gladys Knight and the Pips. Before I knew it, we were on stage. The lights came up, the music started, and Michael began singing. We did "the train," one of the moves that Hector had taught us.

I was surprised at how easy the movements came to me. In just one afternoon my body had gotten used to matching the choreography to the music. I felt loose and comfortable.

Earlier that afternoon, we had not heard Michael sing. We danced to the music on the boom box, not Michael's voice. I was amazed how much he sounded like Gladys Knight. Granted, he looked a little like a linebacker in a dress and wig, but he sounded like Gladys.

As the song went on I looked to my left and noticed that Bird and Kyle were enjoying themselves as much as I was. Kyle in particular was loose-jointed, feeling the music and moving with confidence. He bobbed his head, and pumped his arms to the beat. And every time we'd sing the "whoo, whoo" part in the chorus, and act like we were pulling a train whistle, he'd get a big, goofy grin on his face and look directly at the audience.

When the song ended, we each stood up straight and took a bow in unison, just as we had rehearsed with Hector earlier in the day. The audience applauded loudly and we left the stage. Michael was ecstatic. He hugged each of us and thanked us for helping him.

"I was so nervous," he said, "but I could feel you behind me, and when the music started, I knew we were going to be okay."

While we were backstage, I heard the song "Gloria" playing, and I peeked out to see a guy dressed exactly like Laura Branigan from the music video for the song. She had long dark hair, black spandex pants, and a black top with silver beads and a lightning bolt belt that glittered in the stage lights.

The singer moved just like Branigan did in her music video, complete with hair flips and shoulder shimmies. The problem was that the singer's voice was too low. She couldn't hit some of the notes that Branigan had hit in the song.

"We're heading back out to the table," Bird whispered, tugging on my arm.

We walked to the barroom, where several people congratulated us. Bird walked in front of me and I saw a guy reach out and squeeze his butt. Bird turned around, gave the guy a smile, and playfully slapped his hand. When we got back to the table, Brandy greeted him with a hug that brought her feet off the ground. Everyone was smiling and happy, but there was almost no talking because Laura Branigan was still on stage, singing. When she finished and the audience applauded, Hector leaned over to us and said, "You were all fantastic." For some reason, pleasing Hector felt especially sweet.

"I didn't know you had it in you, man," Martin said.

The MC announced the final contestant of the night. "Singing 'Bette Davis Eyes,' please welcome, Kim Carnes."

The lights came up and the spitting image of Kim Carnes was on stage. It looked so much like Carnes that I thought it might actually be her, until Brian leaned over toward me and said, "That's Rob Worrell. He's really good."

Worrell wore a black pant suit with a white shirt, just like Carnes wore in the video, and she was wearing black sunglasses which she would occasionally slide down her nose seductively as she sang. Her voice was gravelly, just like Carnes's.

When she finished, we ordered another round of drinks and waited for the judges to decide who had won. I didn't care if we won or not. I was just happy for the experience. Even so, I knew how much a win would mean for Michael, so I was holding out hope.

When I looked around, I noticed Kyle was missing, and I asked Brian if he knew where he had gone.

"He went outside with Martin," Brian said. He put his fingers up to his mouth like he was taking a hit from a joint. "He certainly has become fond of pot."

"Yeah, I noticed," I said.

Brandy and Bird stood close together, talking and drinking. I was happy for Bird. He seemed to like Brandy—at least as much as he liked any woman—and it wasn't lost on me that Bird had picked up a woman in a gay bar. That's the kind of luck he had. Throw him in a men's prison and he'd come out dating a female guard.

The music softened and the lights flickered. The judges had made their decision. Kyle and Martin returned to the table just as Marilyn Monroe took the stage.

"Let's thank all of our contestants for their performances this evening." The audience applauded and whistled. "In third place is..." she trailed off until the room became quiet, "Rob Worrell as Kim Carnes." Everyone applauded and the male version of Kim Carnes walked up on stage and stood behind Marilyn Monroe.

"In second place, and I have to say, she looked gorgeous tonight, Michael Hudson as Gladys Knight."

Michael jumped up out of his chair and hugged Hector. When they disengaged, I could see that Hector was crying. Michael went up on stage and stood next to Kim Carnes.

"And the winner of the 1983 Aunt Charlie's Open Mic Competition is…" Marilyn again waited until the room was quiet. "Roger Conrad as Cher."

The first Cher—the one who sang "The Way of Love"—ran up on stage and hugged both Michael and Kim Carnes. The audience stood and cheered. I looked across the table and saw Hector was crying and cheering loudly.

I leaned over toward Brian. "Why are Michael and Hector so happy?" I asked. Second place was nice, but I thought they might be disappointed that Michael hadn't won.

"It's the first time he's ever finished in the top three," Brian said. "This is a really big deal for him."

On stage, Michael leaned forward and said something to Marilyn. Marilyn nodded her head and said into the microphone, "Gladys would like her Pips on stage with her."

Bird, Kyle and I went up on stage to the audience's applause. Kim Carnes and Cher hugged the three of us.

When the onstage festivities ended, we went back to our table and continued celebrating. Michael and Hector were ecstatic. Michael had hugs for everyone at the table, even Martin, who seemed confused by the attention. Hector was especially happy.

"Thank you for your help, amigo," he said. "I had my doubts about you guys, but you pulled it off." He seemed on the verge of tears. He turned, took Michael's arm, and led him onto the dance floor.

When "Open Arms" by Journey started playing, Bird and Brandy went out to dance. She wrapped her arms around his neck and he held her close.

Brian had moved to an adjacent table to talk to two guys I didn't know, and Martin and Kyle had stepped outside again to get high. They invited me, but I begged off. The truth was, I didn't like smoking pot all that much.

The question, "What now?" came into my mind, and it seemed aimed at more than just about the evening and what we were going to do next. I was thinking about my future, including what I was eventually going to do about a job. I thought about the conversation I had with Bird earlier that afternoon. I knew I couldn't tour the country having fun forever. School was over and I'd have to eventually move on. Unlike Kyle, I had never been in a hurry to get out of school and get on with my life. He looked forward to working at his family's bank. The thought of going to work in an office made me feel confined, like a voluntary prisoner in a corporate jail. The thought of working for my father made me feel even worse. I loved my dad, but I feared that working with him would be a disaster. More than anything, I wanted to avoid the typical nine-to-five lifestyle, but I feared it was my fate. Hell, wasn't it everyone's fate?

I watched Bird, and I couldn't help wondering what he was going to do. I was always a little afraid I might become like him. He had no plans for the future and wasn't particularly concerned about it. Maybe I should try to be more like him, not so much irresponsible, but more easy going and carefree. What the hell, it wasn't too late to start now.

My mind was still full of thoughts about the future when I woke up the next morning on Brian's couch. Kyle was asleep in the recliner, still in his tuxedo. I had stripped down to my underwear before going to sleep. My tuxedo lay crumpled on the floor.

"Do you want some breakfast?" Brian asked. He stood in the kitchen with the refrigerator door open. "I'm making eggs."

"Sounds great. Thanks."

Kyle moaned in his chair and pulled the blanket over his head.

"Where's Bird?" I asked.

"He went home with Brandy."

Brian had just finished making scrambled eggs when Bird came into the apartment. He was still in his tuxedo and his hair was spiked at odd angles.

"Good morning, fellow campers."

"Aren't you all chipper this morning," Brian said.

"In fact, I am. How's everyone here?"

"Brian and I have survived," I said. "The jury's still out on Kyle."

Kyle moaned again from beneath the blanket.

"If you want some eggs, I left everything out on the counter," Brian said, pointing toward the kitchen.

"No time," Bird said. "I need to get cleaned up. I have a date this afternoon."

"You and Brandy are really going hot and heavy," I said.

"It's not with Brandy," Bird said. "It's with Megan."

"Who?"

"Megan. You know, the blonde from San Luis Obispo. She's back home in Hayward for the summer and she's coming over to get me. She wants to show me around town."

Bird's news made me sit up on the couch. "How did you get hooked up with her?" I felt a pang of jealousy shoot through me.

"I called her yesterday when we were getting ready to be Pips." Bird ran his hand through his spiky hair.

"She's coming all the way over from Hayward?" Brian asked. "That's on the other side of the Bay."

"She made the offer." Bird shrugged and held his hands out in front of him. "I wasn't going to turn her down."

"I hope you're worth the effort," Brian said.

"I'll do my best," Bird said, smiling his Cheshire cat grin.

§

Bird went out on his date with Megan, and Brian took off to return the tuxedos to the rental place. From there, he planned to meet up with friends for dinner. Kyle and I sat around the apartment all day watching TV. We were both hung over and didn't feel like doing much of anything. By dinner time, we were bored watching MTV videos, so we ventured downstairs to the Vietnamese restaurant.

"I think I'm going to head home," Kyle said.

We had just ordered our food. I got garlic shrimp and Kyle ordered ginger chicken, a dish the waiter recommended.

"Really? When?"

Kyle took a drink of his water, then looked down at the table, drawing invisible patterns with his finger. "I told Joan I'd leave by the weekend. She's been on me about being away so long."

"Kyle, you can't come running every time she feels lonely. You deserve to have some time for yourself."

Kyle looked up from the table and let out a sad laugh. "I know I deserve time for myself, but I don't really want it. I want to be back home. And as far as running to her when she feels lonely, that's what people in relationships do for each other."

I wanted to protest, but I wasn't sure what to say. For my own selfish reasons, I didn't want him to leave. I wanted to avoid adulthood for as I long as I could, and I needed accomplices like Kyle and Bird to go along with me.

"Kyle, you don't have to—"

"There's more to it, Reno." Kyle said. "I snorted cocaine last night and I really liked it." He paused for a moment, touching the condensation on his glass. "That scares the shit out of me. I don't want to do drugs. That's not who I am. I feel like I need to get away from here"

Kyle had snorted coke? Smoking a little pot was one thing, but I knew Kyle well enough to know that he was opposed to hard drugs. Even so, I felt like he was overreacting.

"If you don't want to do coke again, don't do it. You don't have to leave to avoid it."

"I don't want to blame Bird for this," Kyle said, "but I wouldn't be in this position if it wasn't for him. Bad things happen around him. Crazy things. If I wasn't around Bird, I wouldn't have gotten punched in Denver and I wouldn't have done coke last night."

"Was Bird snorting coke, too?"

"No, he wasn't even there. That's not what I mean. It's just, bad shit happens in his wake."

"Don't you think that's kind of unfair?" I asked.

"No, I don't. And I'm afraid if you stay around him, you're going to end up regretting it, too."

There was no sense in arguing with him. If he wanted to go, I couldn't stop him.

The next morning, Bird took Kyle's announcement about leaving in stride. He seemed neither surprised nor angry. "It's been fun," he said when Kyle told him.

"You know that money we got from Candy? I think you guys should use it to buy a car," Kyle said.

"Some of that money is yours," I said.

"You know I don't want any of it. You guys keep it."

Kyle packed his things into his car and drove away from Brian's apartment. He was heading home, and I couldn't help but wonder what was next for Bird and me.

"What now?" I asked Bird. We were sitting in Brian's living room waiting for Brian to get out of the shower.

"The first thing we need to do is get some wheels," he said. "Brian said we could use his car tomorrow to visit dealerships."

"That's fine, but I meant what are we going to do on our Jack Kerouac road trip? I thought we might head down to Mexico like Sal and Dean."

"Don't you want to stay around here for a while?" Bird asked. "I'm really digging San Francisco. This is a great area."

"Yeah, San Francisco's okay, but I didn't think we were going to stay in one spot long term. Aren't we supposed to be having some kind of adventure?"

Bird was playing with a Rubik's cube, turning the faces, but not having any luck getting them to line up. "I have to be honest, Reno. I really like it here. I'm not sure I want to leave."

"You don't think Brian is going to let us live here indefinitely, do you?"

"No, that's why I thought we could get an apartment together."

"Bird, we don't have money for an apartment. Not if we're also going to buy a car."

"We could get jobs. Brandy said she can get me in as a bartender at Vesuvio."

"I don't want a job," I said. "And I don't want to settle down in San Francisco. We were just supposed to be stopping here for a few days." I could feel the anger building inside of me. It was rare for me to get mad at Bird, but he wanted to change everything and expected me to go along with it.

"I know, but I really like it here. I don't want to leave."

Brian stepped into the living room.

"What's going on?" he asked.

"I'm going to take a shower," I said.

I was pissed. This wasn't part of the plan. I didn't like it, but I wasn't sure what to do about it. If Bird was determined to stay in San Francisco, then I'd have to let him stay.

I made the water as hot as I could stand and stood under the spray from the shower. Brian's small bathroom was steamy and the mirror was fogged up. Our road trip was supposed to last for most of the summer. Instead, it had fallen apart in less than two weeks. I was no longer stuck trying to figure out Bird's and Kyle's arguments. Instead, I had to solve my own dilemma.

That night, Bird went to Brandy's, Brian went out with friends, and I stayed at the apartment by myself to read the book Martin had given us as a gift. I wanted to know more about Kerouac because I thought if I knew more about his life, I could figure out where to go next on my Jack Kerouac journey. I might be going alone, but I wasn't ready for it to end.

What I found was that Kerouac was kind of a jerk. He treated people like crap, and was extremely selfish. He yelled at people without provocation, was unmercifully critical, and used others for his own purposes. He was an alcoholic who could be charming one minute, and mean as hell the next. Although he was an interesting character, he wasn't someone I'd want to hang around with.

I also found out that Kerouac lived in Manhattan when he wrote *On The Road*, but had moved to Florida to live with his mother by the time the book was published. He also wrote *The Dharma Bums* at his mother's Florida home.

The next day when Bird came back from Brandy's, I told him I planned on leaving for Florida as soon as I could find a car. I expected him to be angry, but he wasn't. He told me he wanted me to stay, but if I didn't want to, he understood.

We went looking for cars and found two we could afford at a used car dealership just south of San Francisco in Colma. I got a twenty year old VW Van with a pop-up roof, and a back seat that folded into a bed. I thought it would be a great vehicle for an extended road trip. Bird bought a nice, impractical 1968 Cadillac Coupe de Ville convertible. He said it had "style." The dealer agreed to change the oil in both cars since we were buying two at one time.

We only had a few hundred dollars left over, so I called my parents. I concocted a story about having a lead on a good job in Florida. It wasn't exactly a lie. I knew there were jobs in Florida. I just wouldn't know the specifics until I got there. My parents were reluctant at first, but eventually they agreed to wire some money to me.

Brian agreed to let Bird stay with him for a couple more weeks until Bird could put the money together for an apartment of his own. Brandy had offered to let him stay with her, but he declined, claiming he didn't want to put that kind of pressure on their relationship. In truth, Bird wanted to continue seeing Megan, and didn't know how he could see her while living with Brandy.

That night, Bird drove his Caddy across the Bay to see Megan. I stayed home studying maps, figuring out the best way to get to Florida. I thought about what Kyle had said about crazy things happening around Bird. On the one hand, I thought it was unfair of Kyle to blame Bird for his decision to snort cocaine. But I did think he had a point about crazy things happening in Bird's wake.

Bird had a way of barreling through life, drawing the people around him into the chaos. He could be a lot of fun, but he had a bigger than life personality, and a way of sucking all of the oxygen out of a room, leaving precious little air for those around him. Maybe it would do me good to get away from him for a while, to find my own way through the world.

Looking at the maps, I tried to figure out the fastest, most direct route to Florida, but then I changed my mind. I had all summer to kill. I planned a route that took me down the coast through San Diego, then east to Sedona and the Grand Canyon. From there I'd head to Dallas, the Alamo, and Houston. I had heard Padre Island was a lot of fun, so I planned on swinging past there, too. Then on to New Orleans and along the Gulf Coast into Florida, eventually making it to Orlando and Jack Kerouac's mother's house.

I sat on Brian's couch with the map open to the full United States and just stared. There were so many roads out there, so many things to see, so many possibilities. I had a car, a little bit of money, and a whole lot of time. What had happened before didn't matter, and the fate I'd meet at the end of the summer was unimportant too. My whole life was happening right now.

I thought of a line I had read in *On the Road*. I pulled the book out of my backpack, and after a few minutes, found what I was looking for. "The road must eventually lead to the whole world." I read the line out loud, and shouted out like a mad Dean Moriarty, "Yes! Yes! That's right!" I took out a pen and underlined the passage. I was ready to get back on the road and see the whole world.

ACKOWLEDGEMENTS

I'd like to thank the many people who contributed to bringing this book to market. Their support, comments, suggestions, and patience are greatly appreciated.

In particular, I'd like to thank my kids, Shelby and Louis, for their constant love and unselfish support.

Thank you to Melanie Neale, my official editor, and Nick Rupert, my unofficial editor, for all of the time, energy, and patience they provided.

Thank you also to Sean Ironman for his advice, generosity, and expertise when it came to the formatting and aesthetic quality of this book.

I'd like to thank Pat Rushin, Jocelyn Bartkevicius, and David James Poissant for their mentorship, guidance, and support, as well as Amy Beyer, Kate Halma, Cathleen Reed, Andrea Smith Schwebke, Clay Snellgrove, and Sara Penne Villareal for their time, thoughts, and proofreading expertise on this book, and on previous projects.

You all have my highest admiration, and deepest gratitude. Thank you all.

www.ingramcontent.com/pod-product-compliance
Lightning Source LLC
Chambersburg PA
CBHW021017120726
47905CB00009B/3060

* 9 7 8 0 9 9 7 2 4 8 8 0 7 *